PRAISE FOR
DEFINITELY MAYBE

"*Definitely Maybe*, further proof that knowledge can be a dangerous game, is a work of towering wit and intelligence."

—NPR, BEST BOOKS OF 2014

"Like the best speculative fiction, *Definitely Maybe* doesn't show its age: the fundamental questions it addresses are timeless—and effectively and entertainingly framed by the Strugatsky brothers. It remains an intriguing, unsettling work." —*THE COMPLETE REVIEW*

"One of the Strugatsky brothers is descended from Gogol and the other from Chekhov, but nobody is sure which is which. Together they have now proved quite definitely that a visit from a gorgeous blonde, from a disappearing midget, from your mother-in-law, and from the secret police, are all manifestations of a cosmic principle of homeostasis, maybe. This is definitely, not maybe, a beautiful book."

—URSULA K. LE GUIN

"Surely one of the best and most provocative novels I have ever read, in or out of sci-fi." —THEODORE STURGEON

"Provocative, delicately paced and set against a rich physical and psychological background, this is one of the best novels of the year."

—*CHICAGO SUN-TIMES*

PRAISE FOR
ROADSIDE PICNIC

"It's a book with an extraordinary atmosphere—and a demonstration of how science fiction, by using a single bold central metaphor, can open up the possibilities of the novel."

—HARI KUNZRU, *THE GUARDIAN*

"Gritty and realistic but also fantastical, this is a novel you won't easily put down—or forget."   —*109*

"It has survived triumphantly as a classic." —*PUBLISHERS WEEKLY*

PRAISE FOR THE
STRUGATSKY BROTHERS

"The Strugatsky brothers demonstrate that they are realists of the fantastic inasmuch as realism in fantasy betokens a respect for logical consequence, an honesty in deducing all conclusions entirely from the assumed premises."   —STANISŁAW LEM

"[In writing *Gun, with Occasional Music*], I fused the Chandler/Ross MacDonald voice with those rote dystopia moves that I knew backwards and forwards from my study of Ballard, Dick, Orwell, Huxley, and the Brothers Strugatsky."   —JONATHAN LETHEM

"Successive generations of Russian intellectuals were raised on the Strugatskys. Their books can be read with a certain pair of spectacles on as political commentaries on Soviet society or indeed any repressive society."   —MUIREANN MAGUIRE, *THE GUARDIAN*

"Their protagonists are often caught up in adventures not unlike those of pulp-fiction heroes, but the story line typically veers off in unpredictable directions, and the intellectual puzzles that animate the plots are rarely resolved. Their writing has an untidiness that is finally provocative; they open windows in the mind and then fail to close them all, so that, putting down one of their books, you feel a cold breeze still lifting the hairs on the back of your neck."
    —*THE NEW YORK TIMES*

THE DEAD MOUNTAINEER'S INN

ARKADY (1925–1991) and **BORIS** (1933–2012) **STRUGATSKY** were the most acclaimed and beloved science fiction writers of the Soviet era. The brothers were born and raised in Leningrad. Arkady was drafted into the Soviet army and studied at the Military Institute of Foreign Languages, graduating in 1949 as an interpreter from English and Japanese. He served as an interpreter in the Far East before returning to Moscow in 1955. Boris studied astronomy at Leningrad State University, and worked as an astronomer and computer engineer. In the mid-1950s, the brothers began to write fiction, and soon published their first jointly written novel, *From Beyond*. They would go on to write twenty-five novels together, including *Roadside Picnic*, which was the basis for Andrei Tarkovsky's film *Stalker*; *Snail on the Slope*; *Hard to Be a God*; *Monday Begins on Saturday*; *Definitely Maybe*; and *The Dead Mountaineer's Inn*, as well as numerous short stories, essays, plays, and film scripts. Their books have been translated into multiple languages and published in twenty-seven countries. After Arkady's death in 1991, Boris continued writing, publishing two books under the name S. Vititsky. Boris died on November 19, 2012, at the age of seventy-nine. The asteroid 3054 Strugatskia, discovered in 1977, is named after the brothers.

JOSH BILLINGS is a writer and translator who lives in Rockland, Maine. His translations of Alexander Pushkin's *Tales of Belkin* and Alexander Kuprin's *The Duel* were published by Melville House.

JEFF VANDERMEER is an award-winning novelist and editor. His *New York Times*–bestselling Southern Reach Trilogy was named one of *Entertainment Weekly*'s ten best fiction books of 2014, in addition to many other commendations. His fiction has been translated into twenty languages and has appeared in the Library of America's *American Fantastic Tales* and multiple year's-best anthologies. He writes nonfiction for *The Atlantic*, *The New York Times*, *Los Angeles Times*, and *The Guardian*, among other publications.

THE NEVERSINK LIBRARY

I was by no means the only reader of books on board the Neversink. Several other sailors were diligent readers, though their studies did not lie in the way of belles-lettres. Their favourite authors were such as you may find at the book-stalls around Fulton Market; they were slightly physiological in their nature. My book experiences on board of the frigate proved an example of a fact which every book-lover must have experienced before me, namely, that though public libraries have an imposing air, and doubtless contain invaluable volumes, yet, somehow, the books that prove most agreeable, grateful, and companionable, are those we pick up by chance here and there; those which seem put into our hands by Providence; those which pretend to little, but abound in much. —HERMAN MELVILLE, *WHITE JACKET*

THE DEAD MOUNTAINEER'S INN

(ONE MORE LAST RITE FOR THE DETECTIVE GENRE)

ARKADY AND BORIS STRUGATSKY

TRANSLATED BY JOSH BILLINGS
INTRODUCTION BY JEFF VANDERMEER

MELVILLE HOUSE PUBLISHING
BROOKLYN · LONDON

THE DEAD MOUNTAINEER'S INN

Originally published under the title *U Pogibshyego Al'pinista*
Copyright © 1970 by Arkady and Boris Strugatsky
Translation copyright © 2015 by Josh Billings
Introduction copyright © 2015 by Jeff VanderMeer

First Melville House printing: March 2015

Melville House Publishing   8 Blackstock Mews
        145 Plymouth Street   and   Islington
        Brooklyn, NY 11201   London N4 2BT

mhpbooks.com   facebook.com/mhpbooks   @melvillehouse

    Library of Congress Cataloging-in-Publication Data
Strugatskii, Arkadii, 1925–1991, author.
    [Otel' "U pogibshego al'pinista". English]
    The Dead Mountaineer's Inn : (one more last rite for the
detective genre) / Arkady and Boris Strugatsky ; translated
by Josh Billings ; introduction by Jeff VanderMeer.
        pages ; cm
ISBN 978-1-61219-432-5 (pbk.)
ISBN 978-1-61219-433-2 (ebook)
    I. Strugatskii, Boris, 1933–2012, author.   II. Billings, Josh,
1980– translator.   III. VanderMeer, Jeff, writer of introduction.   IV. Title.

PG3476.S78835O8413 2015
891.73'44--dc23

                                                    2014045420

                    Design by Adly Elewa

            Printed in the United States of America
                10 9 8 7 6 5 4 3 2

INTRODUCTION
BY JEFF VANDERMEER

1.

"*Every man wears the face he deserves.*" Or put another way, the mournful cry of "Luarvik L. Luarvik!" from within the besieged Dead Mountaineer's Inn might as well be the mating call of some obscure species of Alps-dwelling penguin. Who is this Mr. Luarvik? Do we believe his version of dire events, or do we believe the hypnotist/motorcycle enthusiast? How about the physicist? Surely a scientist is more objective than a magician! *But how can you be sure when dealing with preternatural events that might just be very imaginative lies?* This is the dilemma facing the earnest but sometimes stumbling detective Peter Glebsky who narrates the novel you hold in your hands. Poor man—he just wanted a vacation away from the family, and instead has to not only solve a crime but also parse varying versions of reality. Back home, he's a cop who covers "bureaucratic crimes, embezzlement, forgery, fraudulent papers." Not exactly someone who deals with . . . *murder*. Much less metaphysics!

Also: Avalanche! Ghosts! Pranks! A lot of creeping around at night!

Confused? Don't be. Think instead of the movie *Clue* or any number of British slapstick mystery-comedies. Perhaps with a hint of *The Twilight Zone*. Because not only does every man wear the face he deserves, but in *The Dead Mountaineer's Inn* the Strugatsky brothers, creators of the Forbidden Zone in their classic science-fiction novel *Roadside Picnic*, give every reader the farce they deserve—with possible infernal devices thrown in to spice up the recipe.

I came to Russian literature through absurdism and dark humor; my encounters with Mikhail Bulgakov's *The Master and Margarita* and Nikolai Gogol's *The Nose* are two of the pivotal experiences of my early adulthood. The idea of a standard, garden-variety realism doesn't figure into this sort of fictional equation. When the Devil's cat in *The Master and Margarita* begins to talk to the corrupt businessman and the businessman argues with the cat for a while before realizing *I am arguing with a talking cat!*, what we're seeing is not just interspecies communication at its most subtle, but one of the classic absurdist scenes in all of fiction. Even in the work of Vladimir Nabokov, you can sometimes see this quality, and the reason it rises again and again in the work I admire—Russian and not-Russian—is that the absurd admits to the illogic of our lives. To the internal inconsistencies that we try to keep in check. When they pile up, that is when comedy or tragedy occurs, as well as the unpredictable. When, in fiction, they spill over into the surreal or fantastical, this is just a psychological extension of what we know to be true in a more mundane sense in our daily lives. Whether we admit it or not.

If Glebsky is upset that he must be "on the job," then in part it may be that he had hoped that the irrationality and absurdity of his normal workweek might be suspended or kept in abeyance while on vacation. But the world doesn't work that way—reality's porous and strange, and we can't ever quite escape it.

The Dead Mountaineer's Inn's finest moments occur at those points where the detective knows less than he thinks he knows, where clues do not add up, where people are acting irrationally and impossible doppelgängers proliferate. Writing explanations is hard, but creating convincing mysteries that are true to the world is more difficult. The Strugatsky brothers as good as tell us this through the inn's owner, Alek Snevar, who says to Glebsky, "Haven't you ever noticed . . . how much more interesting the unknown is than the known? The unknown makes us think—it makes our blood run a little quicker and gives rise to various delightful trains of thought. It beckons, it promises. It's like a fire flickering in the depths of the night."

In support of this treatise, the novel contains one of the better scenes in fiction about waiting in line to use the shower, and not only because there aren't many such scenes in fiction. Glebsky's train of thought as he decides whether or not to wait is a lovely little reverie of indecision. When he realizes there's something odd going on *in* the shower, it's both comic and unnerving because he's been lost in his own thoughts: "He's just here, I remembered. He doesn't drink, he doesn't eat—he just leaves footprints."

The "he" is probably the dead mountaineer, a figure given such a loving and complex mythology by Snevar that even the guests become complicit in propping up the stories. The spirit of the dead mountaineer and the hints of sentience given to the dog that's survived him are just two of the early elements of the novel that delight the reader. (And offset the off-putting weirdness of Glebsky's obsession with the gender of the hypnotist's child and the appearance of the one hackneyed character, a promiscuous maid.)

The Strugatsky brothers clearly loved writing these moments, loved creating a profusion of stories and tales about the stories. There's a jeweler's precision applied to the staging and execution of such scenes—a flair for expressing the foibles of human interaction. Execution's the key; in lesser hands, the legend of the dead mountaineer put forth by the inn's owner would be drab. In lesser hands, the almost *Noises Off* shenanigans on display throughout *The Dead Mountaineer's*

Inn would be sad, unconvincing, louche. It's tough to stage this kind of production. You might spend as much effort on the timing of the inspector Ping-Ponging down corridors to question different suspects as you do mapping the internal logic of a Forbidden Zone. To the writer, all enclosed spaces pose unique challenges, and when you're creating a riff on classic elements like the eccentricities of an inn's staff or the even deeper eccentricities of its guests, your success lies less in originality than in the clarity of the writing.

So: An uncanny moment in a shower. A missing watch. A suitcase that contains . . . what? Do these elements as they assemble capture our imagination—seem most luminous— when mysterious or when explained? Perhaps it depends on the type of tale being told. A mystery with no solution is an irritation to a reader, usually. A science-fiction story with some things left unexplained is to be expected.

When the avalanche roars down, cutting you off from the world, it's just you and characters, and in a sense, you get to choose how to interpret the story

2.

All writers have a border around them: the constraints they have to work against and the way they're perceived by readers. In the case of the brothers, the historical context of their development created an automatic barrier—both for us as English-language readers and for them, existing as they did within a repressive system.

Arkady Natonovich Strugatsky (1925–1991) was born in Batumi but grew up in Leningrad, leaving only during the siege of 1942. He served in the Soviet army, and it was in the Military Institute of Foreign Languages that he became proficient in English and Japanese. From 1955 on, he worked as a writer, and in 1958, he started to collaborate with his brother. Unlike Arkady, Boris Strugatsky (1933–2012) stayed in Leningrad during the siege and then became an astronomer and computer engineer. During the course of their careers, the two brothers would become icons of Russian science fiction, but also of Russian literature in general, although mostly known in Europe. They've never been well known in the United States.

Literary influences on the Strugatsky brothers include Stanisław Lem, who tended toward satire and societal commentary that's not so much funny as tellingly observant. Yet not all literary influences are literary: the siege of Leningrad was among the most brutal events of World War II, and Arkady's flight from the city proved to be its own kind of tragedy: it ended in the death of the brothers' father. But even if they had been shielded from the worst of what happened during the war, it seems unlikely that the deprivation and desperate acts surrounding them could have been without impact. Soviet censorship also was an issue for the brothers, as it was for any honest writer of the time; some of their works did not appear in print until after the fall of the USSR. And in their fiction, over time, relatively optimistic views of the future and of humanity would give way to dystopias, to alienation and a generalized cynicism about human institutions.

Only two years after *The Dead Mountaineer's Inn*, the Strugatsky brothers would publish the iconic *Roadside Picnic*, turned into the classic movie *Stalker* by Andrei Tarkovsky. The two books could not be more different—the latter is an iconic anvil of a book, the former a delicate cobweb of timing and absurdity. *Roadside Picnic* fits perfectly within the brothers' overall body of deeply science-fictional work, while *The Dead Mountaineer's Inn* seems like an amusing one-off—among the last of their works to value pure play above all else.

So where exactly did *The Dead Mountaineer's Inn* come from? In Boris Strugatsky's short memoir *Comments on the Way Left Behind* (Комментарии к пройденному), published

in Russia in 1999, he states that they had wanted to write a detective story (Russian equivalent, "детектив") for some time,
based on a familiarity with Rex Stout, Erle Stanley Gardner,
Dashiell Hammett, John le Carré, and others. This in the context of being aware of a "fundamental vice" of any detective
story: "Two vices, to be precise: first, the pettiness of any criminal motive, and second, the imminence of a boring, disap-
pointingly dull, plausibility-killing, awkward explanation. You
can count all possible motives on the fingers of one hand . . .
Your interest inevitably declines as soon as whos and whys are
revealed."

Thus they strove to create a narrative that, underneath its
seeming whimsy, would be "paradoxical," complete with an
unexpected twist. In 1968, in the midst of writer's block caused
by external pressures—i.e., Soviet censors—they came upon
the solution, in part to "learn to write well but for money,"
even if they later came to see the endeavor as impossible to
achieve due to the inflexibility of mystery-fiction tropes. A
locked-room mystery that wasn't. A whodunit that becomes
something else. Whatever their later reservations, Boris and
Arkady found *The Dead Mountaineer's Inn* "sheer pleasure"
to write—and that pleasure comes across to the reader today.

In the same memoir, Boris recounts how they anticipated
having no trouble publishing *The Dead Mountaineer's Inn*—
originally titled *The Murder Case: Yet Another Requiem for
the Detective Novel*—only to find out to their surprise that
they were wrong, because of prior ideological "misbehavior"
that had created suspicion. "It turned out we had gone too far
with being apolitical and asocial. It turned out that our editors
wished there were some struggles in the novel—class struggle,
struggle for peace, struggle of ideas, just anything."

As a result, when the novel was finally published, the
gangsters in this edition had to be changed to neo-Nazis, a

move the brothers thought was in extreme bad taste. When *The Dead Mountaineer's Inn* was later published as a children's book, a different change had to be made: deleting the mulled wine Glebsky pours into his coffee, since children's books of the time could not mention drinking alcohol. (Eventually, the novel also became a video game and a Russian movie.)

But no matter how the brothers might have been influenced by crime fiction, their science-fictional souls still glimmer darkly upon the fallen snow of the chapters in *The Dead Mountaineer's Inn*, a novel that revels in every kind of tension, that inhabits every available transitional space. The mystery that wants to explain, and the science-fiction story that wants to leave something vague or unexplained: the unexplored horizon, the limits of human understanding. I can almost imagine each brother as the advocate for one of the two causes—the cause of order and the cause of not-order—and only this tussle can create the requisite balance between the two.

Early on, before the two are cut off from the world by an avalanche, the inn's owner says to Grebsky: "But as soon as the unknown becomes known, it's just as flat, gray and uninteresting as everything else."

For the very longest time, the Strugatsky brothers endeavor to make this novel complex and kinetic and fun.

You are about to enter the Dead Mountaineer's Inn.

Are you who you say you are?

Are you *what* you say you are?

What, exactly, will you tell Grebsky when he comes knocking on your door?

THE DEAD MOUNTAINEER'S INN

"Reports from the Vingus region, near the city of Mur, indicate the arrival of a flying machine, from which yellow-green humanoids possessing three legs and eight eyes each have emerged. In their thirst for scandal, the bourgeois press has rushed to call these humanoids visitors from another planet . . ."

(FROM THE NEWSPAPERS)

1.

I stopped the car, got out and took off my sunglasses. Everything was exactly as Zgut had said it would be. The inn was two stories high, a yellowish-green color, with a mournful-looking sign hanging over the front porch that read, "THE DEAD MOUNTAINEER'S INN." Deep spongy snowdrifts on either side of the porch bristled with different-colored skis—I counted seven of them, one with a boot still on it. Knobby dull icicles thick as your arm dangled off the roof. A pale face peered out of the rightmost window on the first floor, and now the front door opened and a bald, stocky man wearing a red fur vest over a dazzling nylon shirt appeared on the porch. He approached with slow, heavy steps and then stopped in front of me. He had a coarse, ruddy face and the neck of a heavy-weight champion. He did not look at me. His melancholy gaze was focused somewhere to the side, expressing a sad dignity. No doubt this was Alek Snevar himself, owner of the inn, the valley surrounding it, and Bottleneck Pass.

"There . . ." he said in an unnaturally low and muffled voice. "It happened over there." He pointed with his hand. There was a corkscrew in it. "On that peak . . ."

I turned, squinting towards the terrifying-looking blue-grey cliff that enclosed the valley to the west: at the pale tongues of snow and the serrated ridge, which looked so

distinct against the sky's deep blue background that it might
have been painted there.

"The carabiner broke," the owner continued in the same
muffled voice. "He fell two hundred meters straight down,
to his death. There was nothing for him to catch hold of on
the smooth rock. Perhaps he cried out. Nobody heard him.
Perhaps he prayed. Only God was listening. When he hit the
cliffs we heard the avalanche here, like the roar of an animal
being woken up: a hungry, greedy roar. The ground shook
as he crashed into it, along with forty-two thousand tons of
powder . . ."

"What was he doing up there?" I asked, staring at the evil-
looking cliff.

"Allow me to immerse myself in the past," the owner said,
bowing his head and laying his fist with the corkscrew in it
against his bald temple.

It was all completely how Zgut had told me it would be,
only I couldn't see a dog anywhere. Still, I noticed a large number of his calling cards lying in the snow near the porch and
around the skis. I climbed back in the car and pulled out the
basket full of bottles.

"Inspector Zgut sends his greetings," I said. The owner immediately emerged from his reverie.

"A wonderful man!" he said in a lively and quite normal-
sounding voice. "How is he?"

"Not bad," I said, handing him the basket.

"I see he hasn't forgotten the evenings he spent here in
front of my fireplace."

"He can't talk about anything else," I said and turned towards the car again—but the owner grabbed my hand.

"Not another step!" he said sternly. "I'll call Kaisa. Kaisa!"
he bellowed.

A dog jumped out onto the porch: a magnificent Saint

Bernard, white with yellow spots, powerful and big as a calf. As I already knew, he was the last remnant of the dead mountaineer, if you didn't count a few scraps on display at the inn's museum. I wouldn't have minded watching this dog with a woman's name unload my bags, but the owner was already steering me towards the house with a strong hand.

As we walked down a dimly lit hall, I caught a whiff of the warm smell of an extinguished fireplace and saw the dull varnished gleam of fashionably low tables; we turned left and the owner shoved his shoulder against a door with the word "Office" on it. Once the jingling, bubbling basket had been installed in a corner, and myself in the comfortable armchair, the owner flung open the huge ledger on his desk.

"Before we begin, allow me to introduce myself," he said, picking at the tip of his fountain pen intently with a fingernail. "Alek Snevar, inn owner and mechanic. Naturally you noticed the wind turbines on your way through Bottleneck?"

"So those were turbines?"

"Yes. Wind-powered engines. I designed and built them with my own two hands."

"Really?" I murmured.

"Yes. By myself. And not just them."

"And where is it going?" asked a shrill female voice behind my back.

I turned around. In the door was a chubby little number holding my suitcase. She was about twenty-five years old, all rouged up and with wide-open, wide-set blue eyes.

"This is Kaisa," the owner explained. "Kaisa! This man brings us greetings from Mr. Zgut. You remember Mr. Zgut, Kaisa? Of course you remember him."

Kaisa blushed instantly and, shrugging her shoulders, covered her face with a hand.

"She remembers," the owner explained to me. "Now she's

getting it . . . Hmmm . . . How about I put you in number four. It's the best room in the inn. Kaisa, take Mr. . . . er . . ."

"Glebsky," I said.

"Take Mr. Glebsky's suitcase to room number four . . . Phenomenally stupid," he explained with a touch of pride, when the little dumpling had stashed herself away. "Remarkable, in her own way . . . So then, Mr. Glebsky?" He stared at me expectantly.

"Peter Glebsky," I recited. "Police Inspector. On leave. For two weeks. Alone."

The owner diligently wrote each of these facts into the ledger in huge gnarled letters; as he wrote the Saint Bernard came in, claws tapping on the linoleum. He looked at me, gave me a wink, and then suddenly, with a roar that sounded like a bundle of firewood collapsing, slumped down near the safe and lay his head on his paw.

"That's Lel," the owner said, screwing the cap of his pen back on. "Sapient. Understands three European languages. No fleas—but he does shed."

Lel sighed and shifted his snout to the other paw.

"Come," said the owner, as he stood up. "I'll show you to your room."

We crossed the hall again and climbed the stairs.

"Dinner is at six," the owner said. "Though you can get a snack anytime, or a refreshing drink for that matter. At ten there's a light supper. Dancing, billiards, cards, conversation around the fireplace."

We went down the corridor on the second floor and turned left. At the very first door the owner stopped.

"Here it is," he said, in that same muffled voice. "After you."

He flung the door open, and I went in.

"Ever since that unforgettable, terrible day . . ." he began, and suddenly grew quiet.

The room didn't look bad, though it was a little gloomy. The curtains were half-drawn; an alpenstock lay on the bed for some reason. There was a smell of freshly smoked tobacco. Someone's waterproof jacket was draped over the back of an armchair; a newspaper was on the floor next to it.

"Hmm . . ." I said, puzzled. "It looks like someone's already staying here."

The owner didn't respond. His eyes were glued to the table. There was nothing out of the ordinary on it, except a large bronze ashtray, in which a straight-handled pipe lay. A Dunhill, I guessed. Smoke rose from the pipe.

"Staying . . ." the owner said eventually. "Well, why not?"

I didn't know what to say to this, so I waited for him to go on. I couldn't see my suitcase anywhere, but there was a checkered rucksack with a bunch of hotel-stickers on it in the corner. It wasn't my rucksack.

"Everything has remained as he left it before his climb," the owner went on, his voice growing stronger. "On that terrible, unforgettable day six years ago."

I looked dubiously at the smoking pipe.

"Yes!" the owner cried. "There's HIS pipe. That's HIS jacket. And that over there is HIS alpenstock. 'Don't forget your alpenstock,' I said to him that very morning. He just smiled and shook his head. 'You don't want to be stuck up there forever!' I shouted, a cold premonition passing over me. '*Porquwapa*,' he said—in French. I still don't know what it means."

"It means 'Why not?'" I said.

The owner nodded sadly.

"That's what I thought," the owner said. "And there's HIS rucksack. I refused to let the police rummage through his things . . ."

"That's HIS newspaper, then," I said. It was clearly yesterday's edition of the *Mur Gazette*.

"No. Of course the newspaper isn't his," the owner said.

"I got that impression too," I agreed.

"The newspaper isn't his, of course," the owner repeated. "And someone else, naturally, has been smoking the pipe."

I muttered something about a lack of respect for the dead.

"Not at all," the owner retorted thoughtfully. "It's much more complicated than that. It's much more complicated, Mr. Glebsky. But we'll talk about that later. Let's get you to your room."

But before we left he peeked into the bathroom, opened the closet door and then closed it again, and walked over to the window. He swatted the curtains a few times. It seemed to me like he wanted to look under the bed too, but restrained himself.

We went out into the hallway.

"I remember Inspector Zgut telling me that he specialized in so-called 'safecrackers,'" the owner said after a short silence. "And may I ask what your specialty is—if it's not a secret?"

He opened the door to room number four for me.

"A boring one," I said. "Bureaucratic crimes, embezzlement, forgery, fraudulent papers . . ."

I liked my room immediately. Everything in it was squeaky clean, the air smelled fresh, the desk was absolutely dust-free, outside the clear window lay a view of the snow-covered valley and purple mountains.

"A pity," the owner said.

"What do you mean?" I asked absently, as I glanced in at the bedroom. Kaisa was still there. She'd opened my suitcase and put away my things, and was busy fluffing the pillows.

"Then again, it's really not a pity at all," the owner remarked. "Haven't you ever noticed, Mr. Glebsky, how much more interesting the unknown is than the known? The unknown makes us think—it makes our blood run a little quicker and gives rise to various delightful trains of thought. It beckons, it promises. It's like a fire flickering in the depths of the night. But as soon as the unknown becomes known, it's just as flat, gray and uninteresting as everything else."

"You're a poet, Mr. Snevar," I remarked, growing more and more distracted. Watching Kaisa, I understood what Zgut had meant. Stretched out against the bed like she was, this dumpling looked pretty tempting. There was something about her, something strange and as yet unknown . . .

"Well, here you are," the owner said. "Settle in, relax, do as you like. Skis, wax, equipment—everything you want can be found downstairs, and if you need anything feel free to contact me directly. Dinner is at six, but if you decide you'd like something to snack on or refresh yourself with right away—I mean drinks, of course—just ask Kaisa. Welcome."

And he left.

As Kaisa continued to work the bed to a level of unimaginable perfection, I took out a cigarette, lit it, and went over to the window. I was alone. At last, thank God in heaven and all his angels, I was alone! I know, I know: you're not supposed to say this kind of thing, or even think it—but how difficult it is in this day and age to get a week, or a day, or even just an hour alone! I mean, I love my children, my wife, I get along well with my family, and the majority of my friends and acquaintances are quite polite and pleasant. But to have them coming around one after the other, and there's no possibility—not even the smallest one—of getting out of it, detaching myself, disconnecting, locking myself away . . . I've never read this myself, but my son maintains that the greatest struggle man faces in the modern world is with solitude and alienation. I don't know. I'm not so sure. Maybe all of this is just a romantic myth, or maybe I'm just unlucky. Either way, for me two weeks of solitude and alienation sounds like exactly what I need. So long as the only things I have to do here are things I want to do, not things I have to do. A cigarette, for example, which I smoke because I want to, not because someone shoved a pack under my nose. And which I don't smoke when I don't want to smoke it—but only because I don't want to, not because Madame Zelts doesn't like the smell of tobacco smoke . . . A glass of brandy by a roaring fire: now that's all right in my book. That would definitely not be a disaster. Apparently things here won't be that bad. Which is just wonderful. I'm doing all right, alone with myself, with my body, which isn't too old yet, it's still strong, I can still put on some skis and dash off, all the way across the valley, towards those purple spikes, over the whistling snow, and then everything will be absolutely perfect . . .

"Can I bring you anything?" Kaisa asked. "Anything you like?"

I looked at her, and once again she shrugged and covered her face with her hand. She was dressed in a close-fitting, multicolored frock, which puffed out in the front and back, and a tiny lace apron. A necklace of large wooden beads hung around her neck. She tilted her feet slightly inward; she didn't look like any of the women I knew. This was also good.

"Who's here right now?" I asked.

"Where?"

"Here. At the inn."

"The inn? Who's staying with us right now? Plenty of people . . .

"Who exactly?"

"Well, let's see. There's Mr. Moses and his wife. They're in one and two. And three—except they're not staying there. Or maybe it's his daughter. It's hard to figure out. She's a beauty, giving them all the look . . ."

"Is that so?" I said, egging her on.

"Then there's Mr. Simone. He's in the room across from yours—a scientist. He's always playing billiards and crawling up the walls. A troublemaker, but dull. Mentally speaking, I mean." She blushed and shrugged her shoulders again.

"Who else?" I asked.

"Mr. Du Barnstoker, the hypnotist who performs in circuses . . ."

"Barnstoker? *The* Barnstoker?"

"I don't know. Maybe. He's a hypnotist . . . And then there's Brun . . ."

"Who's that—Brun?"

"The one who rides the motorcycle in those pants. Another troublemaker, but young."

"Is that all?"

"No, there's someone else. He came not long ago. Only it's just . . . He's just here. He doesn't sleep, he doesn't eat. All we know is that he's here . . ."

"I don't understand," I confessed.

"Nobody understands. He exists—that's all I know. He reads newspapers. The other day he stole Mr. Du Barnstoker's shoes. We looked everywhere, but we couldn't find them. He'd taken them to the museum and left them there. And he leaves footprints everywhere . . ."

"What kind of footprints?" I wanted to understand her.

"Wet ones. Up and down the hallway. And he always calls me. First I get a call from one room, then it's from another. I go, and there's no one there."

"All right," I said with a sigh. "I have no idea what you're talking about, Kaisa. But that's all right. I think I'd better take a shower."

I put out my cigarette in the virginally clean ashtray and went into the bedroom to get underwear. Once there, I put a stack of books on the side-table at the head of the bed, thought briefly that maybe I'd brought them along with me in vain, kicked off my shoes, stuffed my feet into a pair of bathroom slippers, grabbed a bath towel and went to the shower. Kaisa had already left, and the ashtray on the table once again shone with cleanliness and purity. The sound of billiard balls clicking reached me from somewhere down the deserted hallway—that must be the "dull troublemaker." Mentally speaking. What had she said his name was? Simone.

The door to the shower was at the top of the stairs. It appeared to be locked. I stood there indecisively for a few minutes, carefully twisting the plastic doorknob back and forth. Heavy, unhurried steps were coming towards me down the hallway. You could always use the one downstairs, I thought. Or, come to think of it, you could do something else. You could try a few runs on those skis. I stared absentmindedly at the wooden staircase, which appeared to lead all the way up to the roof. Or you could go up on the roof and take a look at the view. They say that the sunsets and sunrises here are indescribably beautiful. And then again, what the hell was with the shower door being locked? Or is someone sitting in there? It's quiet . . . I tried the handle again. All right. Never mind the shower. There's no need to hurry. I turned around and went back.

I could tell immediately that something was different in my room. After a second I understood: there was a smell of pipe smoke, the same one I'd smelled in the inn's museum. I glanced quickly at the ashtray. There was no burning pipe— just a tiny mound of ash with particles of tobacco in it. He's just here, I remembered. He doesn't drink, he doesn't eat— he just leaves footprints.

And then someone nearby yawned loudly. The sound of

clicking claws came lazily from the bedroom, as Lel the St. Bernard gave me a look and then stretched with a grin.

"So you're the one who's been smoking?" I said.

Lel blinked and wagged his head. Like he was shaking a fly off.

2.

Judging by the footprints in the snow, someone had already tried to ski here. They'd made it fifty meters, falling at every step, and then turned around, sunk to their knees by this point, and lugged their skis and poles back, dropping them, picking them back up and dropping them again. Their frost-covered curses had not yet settled over the blue gouges and scars in the snow. But the rest of the snow-covered valley was clean and untouched, like a new starched sheet.

I took a few hops to test the ski bindings, and then sped off with a whoop in the direction of the sun. I increased my pace gradually, squinting from the glare and from pleasure, throwing off with every breath I exhaled the boredom of smoke-filled offices, musty papers, teary perps and grumpy bosses, the stale jokes and tedious political arguments, my wife's petty bustling, the demands of the younger generation . . . The dull, slush-filled streets, the hallways reeking of sealing wax, the empty safes gaping like wrecked tanks, the dining room with its faded blue wallpaper and bedroom with its faded pink wallpaper and the yellowish ink-stained wallpaper of the nursery . . . With every breath I left myself further behind . . . left the tightly wound moralist who followed every law to the last letter, the man whose shirt buttons shone, the attentive husband and exemplary father, hospitable to his friends and friendly with his relatives . . . I was overjoyed to feel all this leaving me, I hoped that it would never return, that from this point forward everything would be light, elastic, crystal-clear, that it would proceed at this same furious, happy, youthful pace, and how good that I'd come here . . . Well done Zgut, clever Zgut, thank you Zgut, although the rumors are that you bust your safecrackers in the chops during interrogations . . . And I'm still that tough, quick, strong—I can do it like that, straight as a razor, a hundred thousand kilometers along a perfectly straight line, or I could do it like this, a sharp right, a sharp left, a ton of snow spraying out from under my skis . . . And then I haven't been on a pair in three years, could it be three years since we bought that damned new house, and what kind of devil made us do that, a place to grow old in, you work all your life to grow old . . . Well damn it, I don't want to think about that, damn old age, damn the house, and damn you Peter, Peter Glebsky, you pencil-pushing clerk, and bless you . . .

When this initial round of enthusiasm had subsided I found myself beside the road, wet, breathing hard, covered from head to foot with powdery snow. Amazing, how quickly the waves of excitement pass. You nag, upbraid yourself for hours and days on end, and then excitement comes—and then it's gone. And now my ears are blocked up because of the wind . . . I took my glove off, stuck a pinky in my ear, twisted and then suddenly heard a crackling roar, as if someone was landing a biplane nearby. I barely managed to wipe my goggles clear before it flew past me—it wasn't a biplane of course: it was a huge motorcycle, one of those new ones that demolish more walls and cost more lives than all the rapists, thieves and murderers combined. It sprayed me with lumps of snow; my goggles slushed up again, but I still managed to pick out the skinny, hunched figure, with its waving black

hair and red scarf sticking out straight as a board behind it. No
helmet, I thought automatically, that's a fifty crown fine and
suspension of your driver's license for a month . . . But there
was no question of making out the license plate—I couldn't
even see the inn, or half of the valley for that matter. Clouds
of snow filled the air. And what do I care anyway? I leaned
into my ski poles and hurried after the motorcycle towards
the inn.

By the time I got there, the motorcycle was cooling down
in front of the porch. Next to it on the snow lay a pair of huge
leather gloves with funnel-shaped sleeves. I thrust my skis
in the snowbank, dusted myself off and took another look
at the motorcycle. It was an evil looking machine. Probably the inn would have to change its name next year to
"The Dead Motorcyclist's Inn." The owner would take his
newly arrived guest's hand and say, pointing at the shattered
wall, "Here. He hit it going a hundred and twenty miles an
hour and kept going until he came out the other side of the
building. The earth shook when he burst into the kitchen
carrying four hundred and thirty-two bricks . . ." What's so
bad about a little advertising, I thought, as I climbed the
stairs. I'll go to my room now and there'll be a skeleton sitting at my desk with a lit pipe between its teeth, and in front
of that skeleton, a bottle of house liquor costing three crowns
a liter.

In the middle of the hall stood a remarkably tall and very
hunched-over man, in a coat whose tails reached to his heels.
He put his hands behind his back as he scolded the scrawny,
floppy-looking creature of indeterminate sex currently loung-
ing in the recliner. The creature had a small, pale face, which
was half-hidden by a pair of huge black sunglasses, a mass of
tangled black hair and a fluffy red scarf.

When I closed the door behind me, the tall man stopped

talking and turned towards me. He was wearing a bow tie and had a noble-looking face, adorned by aristocratic flews and a no-less-aristocratic nose. Only one man had that nose, and this had to be that man. He looked at me for a second as if puzzled, then pursed his lips and walked towards me with a narrow white hand extended in front of him.

"Du Barnstoker." He practically sang it. "At your service."

"Not *the* Du Barnstoker," I asked, sincerely impressed. I shook his hand.

"The very same, sir, the very same," he said. "To whom do I have the honor?"

I introduced myself, feeling a sort of awkward shyness that is quite alien to someone in my line of work. For I could tell immediately that a man like this was certainly hiding his income or lying on his tax returns.

"How charming!" Du Barnstoker sang out suddenly, grabbing me by the lapel. "Where did you find it? Brun, my child, look how charming it is."

He was holding a light blue violet between his fingers. It even started to smell like violets. I forced myself to applaud even though I don't like these kinds of things. The creature in the chair yawned with all of its tiny mouth and threw a leg over the chair arm.

"Up your sleeve," it said in a deep hoarse voice. "Pretty weak, uncle."

"Up my sleeve?" Du Barnstoker repeated sadly. "No, Brun, that would have been amateurish. That would have been utterly weak, as you put it. Not to mention unworthy of a connoisseur such as Mr. Glebsky."

He placed the violet on his palm and looked at it, raising his eyebrows, and then it disappeared. I closed my mouth and shook my head. I was speechless.

"You ski masterfully, Mr. Glebsky," Du Barnstoker said,

"I've been watching you through the window. And I must say, it was truly a pleasure."

"Oh no," I muttered, "It's just a hobby, something I used to do . . ."

"Uncle," the creature called suddenly from the depths of the armchair. "Better make me a cigarette."

Du Barnstoker seemed to remember something suddenly.

"Ah yes!" he said. "Allow me to introduce you, Mr. Glebsky: this is Brun, the sole progeny of my dear departed brother . . . Brun, my child!"

The kid grudgingly hoisted itself up out of the chair and approached. Its hair was luxurious, feminine, or rather maybe not feminine so much as youthful, let's say. Its legs, wrapped in stretchy fabric, were skinny and boyish, or perhaps the opposite: the legs of a shapely young girl. The jacket was three sizes bigger than it needed to be. In short, I would have felt better if Du Barnstoker designated the issue of his dear departed brother as either a niece or nephew. The kid twisted its soft pink mouth into an indifferent smile and extended a chapped, scratched hand.

"Did we scare you?" the creature inquired hoarsely. "There on the road, I mean . . ."

"We?" I asked.

"Well okay, not we exactly. Bucephalus. He's good at that . . . I totally dusted his goggles," it explained to its uncle.

"In this particular case," Du Barnstoker kindly explained, "Bucephalus is not the legendary horse of Alexander of Macedonia. In this particular case, Bucephalus is a motorcycle, an ugly and dangerous machine that has been slowly killing me over the last two years and will in the end, I'm convinced, drive me to my grave."

"Don't forget that cigarette," the kid piped in.

Du Barnstoker shook his head and held out his hands

helplessly. When he clasped them again there was a lit cigarette between his fingers, which he offered to the kid. It in-
haled, grunting capriciously.

"Filtered, as usual . . ."

"Naturally, you'll want a shower after your sprint," Du
Barnstoker said to me. "It's almost time for lunch . . ."

"Of course," I said. "Please excuse me."

I was very relieved to get away from them. I didn't feel
like I was in great form. They'd caught me off guard. All the
same, it seemed to me that a famous magician on stage was
one thing, and a famous magician in his private life was another. I made my exit and made my way up the three flights of
stairs to the floor my room was on.

The corridor was as empty as it had been before. Somewhere billiard balls were still smacking dryly against one
another. The damn shower was still locked. Somehow I managed to clean myself up in my room; I pulled out a cigarette
and collapsed on the couch. I woke to the sound of someone
shrieking and a sinister, throaty laugh coming from the hall. I
jumped up. At that very second there was a knock at the door,
and Kaisa's voice purred, "Dinner is served." I responded posi-
tively, yes, yes, I'm coming, swung my legs off the couch and
stuffed them in my shoes. "Dinner is served!" I heard from a
little ways off, and then again, "Dinner is served!" followed by
the same sharp shriek and ghostly laughter. I even heard the
rattle of rusty chains.

I combed my hair in front of the mirror, meanwhile trying
out a few facial expressions, such as: polite distracted interest,
the manly self-possession of a professional, a simple-souled
openness to any acquaintance, and an aw-shucks grin. None
of these seemed appropriate, so I stopped torturing myself,
dropped a couple of cigarettes in my pocket for the kid and
went out into the corridor. Emerging, I was struck dumb.

The door of the room across from mine was open. A young man was hanging in the doorway, right at the lintel, with his feet jammed against one side of the molding and his back against the other. He actually seemed quite relaxed considering how weird his position was. He looked down at me, flashing long yellow teeth, and gave a military salute.

"Hello," I said, after a second. "Can I help you?"

He jumped down light as a cat and stood in front of me at attention, still holding his salute.

"I salute you, Inspector," he said. "Allow me to introduce myself: Simon Simone, Chief Lieutenant, Cybernetics Division."

"At ease," I said, and we shook hands.

"Actually, I'm a physicist," he explained. "But 'Cybernetics Division' sounds almost as good as 'Infantry.' Kind of funny, actually." Suddenly he burst out with that same terrible sob-laugh, in which one could hear the dampness of dungeons, indelible bloodstains and skeletons in their rusty chains.

"What were you doing up there?" I asked, shaking off my surprise.

"Training," he said. "I'm a mountain climber . . ."

"Dead, or alive?" I said, regretting the joke as soon as he unleashed another avalanche of his gruesome laughter on me.

"Not bad—not bad at all for a first try," he said, wiping his eyes. "No, I'm still alive. I came here to scale the cliffs, but I haven't been able to reach them yet. They're surrounded by snow. So instead I climb the doors, the walls . . ." Suddenly he stopped talking and grabbed my hand. "To be honest," he said, "I came here to recover. I'm worn out. Have you heard of The Midas Project? It's top secret. I've been working on it for four years, without a single vacation. The doctors prescribed a course of sensual indulgence." He laughed again, but we'd reached the dining room by this point and he rushed off

towards the table where the snacks had been laid out. "Follow
my lead, Inspector," he shouted as he ran. "You've got to hurry
if you don't want the dead man's friends and relatives to eat all
the caviar."

The dining room was big, with five windows. In the middle
of it stood a huge oval table with space for twenty people; the
elegant buffet board, blackened with age, sparkled with silver goblets and a large number of mirrors and multicolored
bottles; the tablecloth was starched; the plates were fine por-
celain, the flatware was silver with elegant niello inlay. Still,
things had been set up in the most democratic way possible.
The snack table was covered with . . . snacks. First come, first
served. At another, smaller table, Kaisa was setting out two
delftware tubs filled with vegetable soup and bouillon. Serve
yourself, either one. For those who wanted a drink there
was a battalion of bottles, including brandy, Irish gin, beer
and a house liqueur (made out of Edelweiss petals, Zgut had
claimed).

Du Barnstoker and the progeny of his deceased brother
had already sat down at the table. Du Barnstoker, who was
delicately stirring a bowl of bouillon with a silver spoon,
glared reproachfully at the kid as it planted its elbows on the
table and commenced to devour its vegetable soup.

A dazzling, uncommonly beautiful woman who I didn't
recognize was holding court at the head of the table. She was
somewhere between twenty and forty years old, with soft,
dusky-blue shoulders, a swan-like neck, huge, half-closed eyes
with long eyelashes, voluminous ash-blond hair and a tiara
that looked like it cost a fortune. The woman was so out of
place at this simply set inn table that I knew she had to be Mrs.
Moses. I had never seen a woman like her, except in glossy
magazines and maybe at the movies.

The owner, who had a tray in his hand, skirted the table on

his way towards me. On this tray was a crystal glass glowing with an eerie blue liqueur.

"Trial by fire!" he announced when he reached me. "I'd grab something spicy."

I did what he said. I made myself a plate of olives and caviar. I looked at the owner and added a pickle. Then I looked at the liqueur and squeezed half a lemon over the caviar. Everyone was watching me. I took a glass, exhaled (there went another couple musty offices and corridors) and poured the liqueur into my mouth. I shuddered. Everyone was looking at me, so I shuddered only on the inside, and bit off half the pickle. The owner grunted. Simone also grunted. Mrs. Moses said, in a crystalline voice, "Now there's a real man." I smiled and tucked the second half of the pickle into my mouth, bitterly regretting the fact that there were no melon-sized pickles available. "Cool!" the kid said distinctly.

"Mrs. Moses!" the owner said. "Allow me to introduce Inspector Glebsky."

The ash-blond tower at the head of the table swayed slightly, the extraordinary eyelashes rose and lowered.

"Mr. Glebsky!" the owner said. "Mrs. Moses."

I bowed. I would have gladly doubled over, my stomach was hurting so much, but Mrs. Moses smiled, and I soon started to feel better. Turning away shyly, I finished off my appetizers and started on the soup. The owner sat me across from the Barnstokers, putting Mrs. Moses to my right—too far away, unfortunately—and to my left—unfortunately too close—Simone the dull fool, who looked ready at any moment to let loose with his ghoulish laughter.

The owner directed the table's conversation. We talked about mysterious and unknown things—to be precise, about the strange events that had been happening at the inn over the last couple of days. Since I was new to this, they filled me in on the details. Du Barnstoker confirmed that, as a matter of fact, two days ago he had lost a pair of shoes, which were discovered that evening in the inn's museum. A chuckling Simone explained that someone had been reading his books, most of which were on scientific topics, and making notes in the margins. The majority of them were utterly ignorant. The owner, overcome with pleasure, mentioned what had happened today with the lit pipe and the newspaper, adding that he was certain someone wandered the building at night. He had heard them with his own ears, and one time even saw a white figure making its way across the hallway from the front door to the stairs. Mrs. Moses willingly confirmed these reports, adding that yesterday night someone had been staring at her through the window. Du Barnstoker likewise seconded the fact that someone roamed the building at night, but added that he thought it was only good old Kaisa—at least, that's what he thought. The owner remarked that this was completely impossible, while Simon Simone bragged that he slept like the dead and didn't hear a thing at night. Nevertheless, he had noticed twice already that his ski boots were constantly wet, as if someone were running around in them in the snow at night. To amuse myself, I chimed in with the story of the ashtray and the St. Bernard, at which point the kid hoarsely announced to everyone that it, the kid that is, had nothing in general against all this weirdness, it was used to such hocus-pocusy stuff, but couldn't stand it when strangers decided to lay down in its, that is the kid's, bed. Upon saying this it pointed its sunglasses fiercely in my direction, making me glad that I had only just arrived today.

The atmosphere of self-indulgent spookery hanging over the table was broken by the physicist.

"So a captain arrives in an unfamiliar city," he announced. "He checks into his hotel and says he wants to speak to the owner . . ."

Suddenly he stopped and looked around.

"Excuse me," he said. "I had forgotten that I was in the presence of a lady." Here he bowed in the direction of Mrs. Moses. "Not to mention a young . . . er . . . a youth." He stared at the kid.

"I've heard this one," the kid said with disdain. "'It's good, but you can't split it.' Is it that one?"

"Exactly," Simone said, and let loose a burst of laughter.

"What can you split?" Mrs. Moses said, smiling.

"You *can't* split it!" the kid corrected her angrily.

"Ah: you *can't* split it," a surprised Mrs. Moses said. "But what aren't we splitting?"

The kid opened its mouth to respond, but Du Barnstoker made a subtle gesture, and a large red apple appeared there. The kid immediately took a juicy bite out of it.

"The bottom line is that amazing things don't just happen in our inn," Du Barnstoker said. "One has only to recall, for example, the unidentified flying objects . . ."

The kid pushed its chair back with a crash, stood up and, still munching on the apple, made its way to the exit. Well I'll be damned—for suddenly I seemed to be watching the slender figure of a charming young woman. But as soon as my heart softened the young woman vanished, leaving behind her, in the most obscene way, a brash and impertinent teenager: the kind that spread their fleas over beaches and shoot drugs in public bathrooms. Was it a boy? Or, damn it, a girl? I had no idea who to ask, and meanwhile Du Barnstoker was prattling on:

"Gentlemen: Giordano Bruno was burned for a reason. Doubtless, we are not alone in the universe. The only question is how densely intelligence is distributed through space. According to various scholars' estimates—Mr. Simone will correct me if I'm mistaken—there may be up to a million inhabited solar systems in our galaxy alone. If I was a mathematician, gentlemen, I would, on the basis of this fact alone, attempt to establish at least the probability that our Earth is the object of someone else's scientific attention . . ."

I thought it over: to ask Du Barnstoker himself would be somewhat awkward. Besides, maybe even he doesn't know. A kid is a kid . . . No doubt my gracious host couldn't care less. Kaisa's dumb. To ask Simone would be to bring his undead laughter back to life . . . But then what am I doing? Why do I care? Should I grab more roast? Kaisa is dumb, that's for certain, but she knows a lot about cooking . . .

"You must agree," Du Barnstoker murmured, "The idea that alien eyes are attentively and diligently studying our little corner of the universe across the cosmic abyss—this idea alone is enough to capture the imagination . . ."

"By my calculations," Simone said. "The probability that they would be able to distinguish the areas settled by humans from the uninhabited ones, and then pay attention only to the inhabited parts, is e to the negative first power."

"Is that so?" Mrs. Moses said, letting out a reserved gasp as she granted Simone a delighted smile.

Simone broke into his hee-haw. His eyes even started to water and he squirmed in his chair.

"How much is that in real numbers?" Du Barnstoker asked, after weathering this acoustic attack.

"About two thirds," Simone said, wiping his eyes.

"But that's a huge probability," Du Barnstoker said warmly. "As I understand it, that means that we are almost certainly an object of observation!"

At this point the door to the dining room creaked and rattled behind me, as if leaned against with great force.

"Pull!" the owner shouted. "Pull, please!"

I turned around at the exact moment that the door opened.

An astonishing figure stood on the threshold: a massive older man with a face that looked exactly like a bulldog's, dressed in a sort of hilarious, salmon-colored waistcoat straight out of the middle ages, whose hem hung all the way to his knees. Under this doublet, I could see uniform pants with golden general's stripes. One of his hands was pressed against his back, and the other was holding a tall metal mug.

"Olga!" he growled, staring straight ahead with bleary eyes. "Soup!"

A brief hubbub erupted. Mrs. Moses threw herself towards the soup table with uncharacteristic haste, the owner pulled himself from the buffet table and began gesturing with his hands, as if to signal his readiness to provide any service, Simone hurriedly stuffed his mouth with potatoes and rolled his eyes in order to avoid breaking out in laughter, while Mr. Moses (it had to be him) ferried his mug and solemnly quivering cheeks to a chair beside Mrs. Moses, where he sat down, practically missing his seat.

"It's snowing out, gentlemen," he announced. He was completely drunk. Mrs. Moses set his soup in front of him; he stared sternly at the dish and took a sip from his mug. "What's everyone been talking about?"

"We've been discussing the possibility of visitors from another planet here on earth," Du Barnstoker explained, smiling agreeably.

"What do you mean?" asked Mr. Moses, glaring suspiciously over his mug at Du Barnstoker. "I did not expect this from you, Barn . . . Bardel . . . Dubel . . ."

"Oh, it's only a theory," Du Barnstoker said casually. "Mr. Simone has calculated the odds for us."

"Nonsense," Mr. Moses said. "Rubbish. Mathematics—now there's a science . . . And who is this?" he asked, rolling his right eye at me. It seemed murky somehow, a bad eye.

"Allow me to introduce you," the host said hurriedly. "Mr. Moses, Inspector Glebsky. Inspector Glebsky, Mr. Moses."

"Inspector," grumbled Moses. "Fake documents, forged passports . . . I'll have you know my passport is not a forgery, Glebsky. Is your memory any good?"

"I can't complain," I said.

"Well, then, don't forget that." He glared sternly at his bowl again and took a sip from his mug. "Good soup today," he said. "Olga, take this away and bring me some sort of meat. But why have you stopped talking, gentlemen? Continue, continue, I will listen."

"Yes, meat, that reminds me," Simone piped up. "A glutton walked into a restaurant and ordered a filet . . ."

"A filet—what's wrong with that?" Mr. Moses said approvingly, as he tried to cut his roast with one hand. He did not remove the other hand from its mug.

"The waiter said he would bring one right away," Simone continued. "And the glutton stared up at the girls on the stage while he waited . . ."

"Hilarious," Mr. Moses said. "So far, utterly hilarious. This needs salt—Olga, pass the salt. Well?"

Simone hesitated.

"Excuse me," he said uncertainly. "I'm having very serious apprehensions about the present company."

"So? Apprehensions," Mr. Moses announced with satisfaction. "What happened next?"

"That's it," Simone said dolefully. He leaned back in his chair.

Moses stared at him.

"What do you mean 'That's it'?" he asked indignantly. "He brought him the filet, didn't he?"

"Well . . . actually . . . no, he didn't," Simone said.

"What impertinence," Moses said. "He should have called

the *maître d'.*" He pushed his plate away in disgust. "That was an unpleasant story you told us, Simone."

"I guess it is," Simone said, smiling faintly.

Moses took a sip from his mug and turned to the owner.

"Snevar," he said. "Have you found the miscreant who's been stealing our shoes? There's a job for you, Inspector. You can pursue it in your spare time—come to think of it, you're not doing anything at the moment. Some miscreant has been stealing shoes and looking in people's windows."

I was about to reply that I would absolutely look into it; but just then the kid started Bucephalus's engine right underneath the window. The glass in the dining room shook, making conversation impossible. Everyone buried themselves in their plates as Du Barnstoker, pressing his splayed fingers against his heart, poured out muted apologies to his right and left. Then Bucephalus's roar became completely unbearable; clouds of light snow soared past the windows; the roar quickly moved away, fading into a barely audible hum.

"Just like Niagara Falls," the crystalline voice of Mrs. Moses rang out.

"Or a rocket launch!" Simone said. "Awful machine."

Kaisa approached Mr. Moses on tiptoe, and set a decanter of pineapple syrup in front of him. Moses gazed favorably at it before taking a sip from his mug.

"And what do you think about this thievery, Inspector?" he said.

"I think someone here has been playing jokes," I answered.

"There's an odd idea," Moses said disapprovingly.

"Not really," I retorted. "First of all, none of these activities appear to have any goal other than confusion. Second, the dog isn't acting like there are strangers here."

"Oh yes," the owner said in a hollow voice. "Of course, no

one in this house is a stranger to him. But HE wasn't just 'not a stranger' to my Lel. HE was his god, gentlemen!"

Moses stared at him.

"Who is this 'HE'?" he asked sternly.

"HE. The dead mountaineer."

"How fascinating!" Mrs. Moses chirped.

"Don't fool around with my head," Moses told the host. "And if you know who's behind these events, then advise him—strongly advise him!—to stop. Understand me?" He turned his bloodshot eyes at us. "Otherwise I'll start pulling some practical jokes of my own!" he snapped.

Everyone was silent. It seemed to me that they were all trying to imagine what a practical joke from Mr. Moses would look like. I didn't know about the others, but personally I didn't think anything good would come out of it. Moses stared down each of us in turn, not forgetting to take a sip from his mug as he did so. It was completely impossible for me to tell who he was and what he was doing here. And why was he wearing that ridiculous coat? (Perhaps he had already started joking with us?) And what did he have in that mug? And how come it always seemed full, even though, to my eyes, he had already taken around a hundred sips from it—deep ones, too?

Mrs. Moses set down her plate, applied a napkin to her beautiful lips and, raising her eyes to the ceiling, said:

"Oh how I love beautiful sunsets! What a feast of colors!"

I immediately felt a strong desire to be alone. I stood and said firmly:

"Thank you, ladies and gentlemen. I'll see you at dinner."

3.

"I have no idea who he is," the owner said, examining his glass under the light. "He signed the book claiming to be a salesman traveling for personal reasons. But he's no salesman. A half-crazy alchemist, magician, inventor maybe . . . but not a salesman."

We were sitting in front of the fireplace. The coals were hot; the armchairs ancient, sturdy, reliable. The port was warm, infused with lemon, and fragrant. The low light was comfortable, ruddy, utterly cozy. A blizzard was whipping itself up outside and causing the fireplace to whistle. The inn was quiet, except for the peal of sobbing laughter that burst out every once in a while, as if from a cemetery, accompanied by the clack of a well-shot billiard ball. Kaisa was banging pans together in the kitchen.

"Salesman are usually cheap," the owner continued thoughtfully. "But Mr. Moses is not cheap—not at all. 'Might I ask,' I asked him, 'Whose recommendation I have to thank for the honor of your stay?' Instead of answering me he took a hundred-crown bill out of his pocket, set fire to it with his lighter, then lit a cigarette off of that and answered, blowing smoke in my face: 'The name is Moses, sir. Albert Moses! A Moses doesn't require a recommendation. A Moses is at home everywhere and under every roof.' What do you think of that?"

I thought about it.

"I know a counterfeiter who said the exact same thing when asked for his papers," I said.

"Impossible," the owner said smugly. "His bills are real."

"Some kind of insane millionaire, then?"

"He's definitely a millionaire," the owner said. "But who is he? He's traveling for personal reasons . . . But no one just passes through my valley. People come here to ski or rock climb. It's a dead end. It doesn't go anywhere."

I leaned back in the chair and crossed my legs. It felt unusually good to be sitting in exactly this position and speculating, in the most serious possible manner, on the identity of Mr. Moses.

"Well, all right, then," I said. "A dead end. And what is someone like Mr. Du Barnstoker doing at this dead end?".

"Oh, Mr. Du Barnstoker—he's another matter altogether. He's been visiting me every year now for thirteen years. The first time he came, the inn was still known as 'The Shack.' He's crazy for my liqueur. Mr. Moses, on the other hand, appears to be constantly drunk—but he hasn't asked me for a single bottle."

I grunted significantly and took a large sip.

"An inventor," the owner said decisively. "An inventor, or a magician."

"You believe that there are such things as magicians, Mr. Snevar?"

"Please, call me Alek. Plain Alek."

I picked up my glass and toasted Alek with another long swallow.

"In that case, call me Peter," I said.

The owner nodded solemnly and took a generous sip in Peter's honor.

"Do I believe in magicians?" he said. "I believe in anything that I can imagine, Peter. In wizards, in almighty God, in the devil, in ghosts, in flying saucers. If the human brain is capable of imagining something, then that means it must exist somewhere—otherwise why would the brain be capable of imagining it?"

"You're a philosopher, Alek."

"Yes, Peter, I'm a philosopher. I'm a poet, a philosopher, a mechanic. Have you seen my perpetual motion machines?"

"No. Do they work?"

"Sometimes. A lot of the time I have to stop them, their parts wear out way too fast . . . Kaisa!" he yelled, so suddenly that I was startled. "Another glass of hot port for Mr. Inspector!"

The St. Bernard came in, sniffed us, gazed skeptically at the fire, retreated to the wall and fell on the floor with a thud.

"Lel!" the host said. "Sometimes I envy that dog. He sees and hears a lot—quite a lot—as he wanders the halls at night. He could probably tell us quite a story, if he was capable of doing it. And if he wanted to, of course."

Kaisa appeared, looking very flushed and slightly disheveled. She handed me the glass of port, curtsied, giggled and left.

"What a little dumpling," I muttered mechanically. After all, I was on my third glass. The owner laughed good-naturedly.

"She's irresistible," he confessed. "Even Mr. Du Barnstoker couldn't restrain himself. He pinched her bottom yesterday. And the reaction she gets from our physicist . . ."

"In my opinion, our physicist has his eye primarily on Mrs. Moses," I said.

"Mrs. Moses . . ." the host said thoughtfully. "You know, Peter, I have good reason to suspect that she is neither a Mrs. nor a Moses."

I didn't object to this. Who cares, anyway . . .

The owner continued. "No doubt you've already noticed that she is significantly dumber than Kaisa. Not to mention the fact that"—he lowered his voice—"Moses beats her. In my opinion."

I shuddered.

"What do you mean 'beats?'"

"In my opinion, he uses a whip. Moses has a whip. A quirt. As soon as I saw it I thought, 'Now why would Moses need a quirt?' Can you answer that one for me?"

"But Alek . . ." I said.

"I'm not prying," the owner said. "I never pry, about anything. As for Mr. Moses, you brought him up—I would never have allowed myself to bring up that particular subject. I was speaking of our illustrious physicist."

"All right," I agreed. "Let's talk about the illustrious physicist."

"This is the third or fourth time he's stayed with me," the owner said. "Each time he visits, he's more illustrious."

"Wait," I said. "Who are we actually talking about?"

"Mr. Simone, obviously. Don't tell me you've never heard of him?"

"Never," I said. "Why would our paths have crossed—because of some forged baggage documents?"

The owner gave me a reproachful look.

"One should know the heroes of one's national science," he said sternly.

"You're serious?" I said.

"Absolutely."

"That pesky little bore—a hero of our national science?"

The owner nodded.

"Yes," he said. "I know what you mean: the way a man carries himself is the most important thing, everything else is secondary. No doubt you're right. Mr. Simone has provided me with an inexhaustible source of reflection on the glaring discrepancy between a man's behavior when he's relaxing, and the value for humankind of that same man when he's at work."

"Huh," I said. It was worse than the quirt.

"I see that you don't believe me," the owner said. "But I must say . . ."

He paused, and I sensed that there was someone else with us by the fireplace. I had to turn my head and squint. It was the only child of Du Barnstoker's deceased brother. The kid had snuck up to us without making a sound, and now it was squatting next to Lel and stroking the dog's head. Bright red light from the glowing coals was playing in its huge black glasses. The kid somehow seemed very lonely, forgotten and small. It gave off a barely perceptible smell of sweat, high-quality perfume and gasoline.

"What a blizzard . . ." it said in a plaintive and reedy voice.

"Brun," I said. "Hey, kid, take off those awful glasses for a minute."

"Why?" the kid asked drearily.

Why indeed, I thought, and said:

"Because I'd like to see your face."

"That is absolutely unnecessary," the child said, sighing, and asked: "Please give me a cigarette."

Well, then, it was obviously a girl. A very sweet girl. And very lonely. How awful: to be by yourself at her age. I took out a pack of cigarettes for her and flicked open my lighter, searching for something to say but not finding anything.

Of course it was a girl. She even smoked like a girl: in short, nervous puffs.

"I'm scared," she said. "Someone was fiddling with the doorknob to my room."

"There, there," I said. "It was probably just your uncle."

"No," she said. "My uncle is asleep. He dropped his book on the floor and just lay there with his mouth open. For some reason I suddenly thought he'd died . . ."

"A glass of brandy, Brun?" the owner said in a muffled voice. "No harm in a little glass of brandy on a night like this."

"I don't want any," Brun said and shrugged her shoulders. "Are you going to be sitting here much longer?"

I lacked the strength to go on listening to her pitiful voice any longer.

"What the hell, Alek," I said. "Are you the owner of this establishment or not? Couldn't you order Kaisa to spend the night with this poor girl?"

"That's a good idea," the kid said, perking up. "Kaisa—that's just what I need. Kaisa, or something like that."

I drained my glass in confusion, as the kid shot a long and precise strand of spit into the fireplace and flicked her stub in after it.

"There's a car outside," it said in a husky baritone. "Can't you hear it?"

The owner stood up, picked up his fur vest and headed for the exit. I ran after him.

A real blizzard was raging outside. A large black car was idling in front of the porch. The beams of its headlights lit up people arguing and waving their arms.

"Twenty crowns!" screeched a falsetto voice. "Twenty crowns and not a penny less! Damn you—didn't you see the road?"

"For twenty crowns I could buy you and that clunker both!" someone screamed back.

The owner rushed off the porch.

"Gentlemen!" he bellowed loudly. "What is this foolishness?"

"Twenty crowns! I still have to make it back!"

"Fifteen crowns and not a penny more! Extortionist! Give me your license number—I want to write it down!"

"You're a cheapskate through and through! Ready to kill yourself over a fiver!"

"Gentlemen! Gentlemen!"

I was starting to get cold, so I went back to the fireplace. Neither the kid nor the dog were there anymore. This disappointed me. I picked up my glass and made my way to the bar. In the hall, I stopped; the front door burst open, revealing a huge, snow-covered man carrying a suitcase. "Brrr . . ." he said, shaking himself until a blond, red-cheeked Viking was standing before me. His face was wet, and snow lay on his eyebrows in white tufts. When he saw me, he smiled briefly, displaying his even, clean teeth, and said, in a deep and pleasant voice:

"Olaf Andvarafors. Just Olaf is fine."

I introduced myself too. The door blew open again, letting in the owner carrying two trunks, and behind him a small man bundled up to his eyeballs, who was also covered with snow, and very upset.

"Damned crooks!" he said, in hysterical anguish. "We'd agreed on fifteen. Seven and a half a head, that's just obvious—so where'd twenty come from? What the hell is wrong with the people in this town? For Christ's sake, I'll drag him to the station! . . ."

"Gentlemen, gentlemen!" the host said. "All this over a trifle . . . I beg you, this way . . . Gentlemen! . . ."

The small man continued to shout about bloody mugs and the police, as he allowed himself to be dragged away to the office—at which point Olaf the Viking boomed, "What a scrooge . . . ," looking around as if he were surprised not to find a crowd here waiting to greet him.

"Who was that?" I asked.

"I don't know. The taxi picked us both up—there wasn't another one."

He stared silently at a point somewhere above my shoulder. I looked around: there didn't seem to be anything remarkable there. Just a curtain drawn across the entrance to the corridor that led to the study and the Moseses' room. It was swaying slightly, probably from the draft.

4.

By morning the storm was over. I got up at dawn, while the rest of the inn was still asleep; I rushed out onto the porch wearing only my underwear, and scrubbed myself all over with fresh, fluffy snow, in the hope of getting rid of the hangover I was still feeling from the three glasses of port. The sun had just risen from over the eastern ridge, and the long blue shadow of the inn was stretching into the valley. I noticed that the third window to the right on the second floor was wide open. Apparently someone couldn't get enough of the healthy mountain air—even at night.

I went back to my room, got dressed, locked the door behind me and ran to the pantry, practically jumping down the stairs. A flushed and sweaty Kaisa was already fussing over the lit stove in the kitchen. She brought me a cup of cocoa and a sandwich, both of which I finished standing right there in the pantry, as I listened with half an ear to the owner humming away in his workshop. Please let me not run into anyone, I thought. This morning is too good to share . . . Thinking about it—about the clear sky, the golden sun, the empty, powder-filled valley—I felt like a miser, like the little man who'd appeared last night in that fur coat up to his eyebrows, ready to get in a fight over five crowns (Hinkus was his name, a youth counselor: he was on sick leave.) And then wouldn't you know

it, I didn't run into anyone, except Lel the St. Bernard, who
watched with good-natured indifference as I buttoned my
bindings and sped off into a morning, a bright sky, a golden
sun, a fluffy white valley that were all mine.

After finishing a ten-mile ski to the river and back, I returned to the inn to grab a bite to eat and found that things
were already in full swing. The inn's inhabitants emerged en
masse to warm themselves in the sun. The kid and Bucephalus
were eviscerating the fresh snow drifts, to the delight of on-
lookers. Steam rose off both of them. The now coatless youth
counselor, who turned out to be a sharp-faced and emaci-
ated type in his mid-thirties, was hooting as he traced figure
eights around the inn—though never venturing too far out.
Even Mr. Du Barnstoker had perched himself on a pair of skis
and was already so coated in snow that he looked like a weary
and incredibly tall snowman. As for Olaf the Viking, he was
practically dancing on his skis. I felt pang of jealousy when I
saw that he was a real master. Mrs. Moses in an elegant fur
cape looked down over everything from the inn's flat roof, as
did Mr. Moses with his waistcoat and inevitable mug, and the
owner, who was explaining something to them both. I looked
around for Mr. Simone. The great physicist had to be around
here somewhere—I had heard his barking neigh from three
miles away. And there he was: saluting me from the top of a
totally smooth telephone pole.

People greeted me very warmly, for the most part. Mr. Du
Barnstoker informed me that I appeared to have a worthy new
rival, and Mrs. Moses shouted from the roof, in her voice like
the tinkling of silver bells, that Mr. Olaf was gorgeous: a virile
god of a man. This annoyed me; so I wasted no time making a
complete fool of myself. When the kid (who was clearly a boy
today: a kind of wild angel, devoid of manners or morals) pro-
posed a race on skis dragged behind his motorcycle, I decided

to defy both fate and the Viking, and was the first to pick up the end of the cable.

A dozen years ago races like this had been a piece of cake for me—but that was before the industrialized world had come up with Bucephalus, and anyway, back then I'd been stronger. To make a long story short, three minutes later I found myself in front of the porch. I must not have looked so hot, because I heard Mrs. Moses ask in a frightened voice if I needed to be rubbed with snow. Mr. Moses wondered grimly if anyone knew of a substance that could rub out the memory of my disastrous skiing; meanwhile the owner quickly appeared, carefully hoisted me under the arms and began trying to convince me to swallow a swig of his personal magical elixir. "It's fragrant, strong, and will relieve pain and restore peace of mind." Mr. Simone bellowed and whooped sarcastically from the top of the telephone pole; Mr. Du Barnstoker, apologizing, held a handsworth of splayed fingers against his heart. Hinkus the youth counselor excitedly jostled his way to the front of the crowd and whipped his head around, asking everyone if I'd broken any bones, and "where they'd taken him."

They brushed me off, patted me down, massaged me, wiped my face, dug the snow out from underneath my collar and looked around for my helmet, as Olaf Andvarafors grabbed the end of the cable . . . at which point they threw me aside and turned their attention to this new wonder, which truly was quite spectacular. I was surprised how quick the turnaround was: I hadn't even finished picking myself up before the crowd began hoisting their new hero. But fortune doesn't care whether you're a blond snow-god or an aging police officer. At the height of his triumph, when the Viking was already towering over the porch, leaning picturesquely on one ski pole as he smiled dazzlingly at Mrs. Moses, fortune gave her wheel a little tap. Lel the St. Bernard made his way to the winner, gave him an intent sniff and then suddenly, with a quick, precise gesture extended his right paw out directly over his ski boots. I couldn't have scripted it better myself. Mrs. Moses screamed, the crowd burst into a series of hearty curses, and I went back inside. I am not a gloating man by nature, but I love justice. In everything.

Back in the pantry I discovered from Kaisa (with no small difficulty) that the inn's showers, as it turned out, were working only on the first floor: I ran for fresh towels and underwear, but despite my haste I was too late. The shower had already been taken; the sound of rippling water and garbled singing emerged from behind the door, in front of which Simone stood, with his own towel draped over his shoulder. I took my place beside him; Du Barnstoker soon appeared beside me. We started smoking. Simone, choking with laughter as he looked around, started to tell a joke about a bachelor who moved in with a widow and her three daughters. Fortunately, however, Mrs. Moses appeared at exactly that moment and asked us whether we'd seen her lord and master Mr. Moses walking by. Mr. Du Barnstoker replied gallantly, and at length: no, alas. After licking his lips, Simone stared at Mrs. Moses with languid eyes, as I listened to the voice coming from the shower—suggesting finally that Mr. Moses might be found inside. Mrs. Moses received this suggestion with obvious skepticism. She smiled, shook her head and explained to us that in their house on the Rue de Chanelle, they had two bathrooms—one made of gold, and the other, I believe, made of platinum; having struck us dumb with this information, she told us that she would go look for Mr. Moses elsewhere. Simone immediately offered to go with her, leaving Du Barnstoker and myself behind. Lowering his voice, Du Barnstoker asked if I had witnessed the unfortunate scene that had taken place between Lel the St. Bernard and Mr. Andvarafors. I allowed myself the small pleasure of telling him that I hadn't. At which point Du Barnstoker related the scene to me in full detail and, when I had finished throwing my hands up and clicking my tongue sadly, added mournfully that our good host had completely lost control over his dog, for only a day earlier the St. Bernard had relieved himself in the exact same way on Mrs. Moses herself in the garage. Once more, I threw my hands in the air and clucked my tongue (sincerely this time) but just then we were joined by Hinkus, who immediately started complaining about the fact that he was paying double the normal amount for a room in an inn with only one working shower. Mr. Du Barnstoker calmed him down by removing from within the folds of his towel a pair of lollipops shaped like roosters. Hinkus grew immediately quiet; his face changed completely, the poor man. He took the roosters, stuffed them into his mouth and stared at the great prestidigitator in horror and disbelief. Then Mr. Du Barnstoker, looking extremely pleased at the effect he'd produced, proceeded to entertain us with the multiplication and division of multidigit numbers.

Meanwhile the shower water continued to beat down, though the singing had been replaced now by unintelligible muttering. From the top of the stairs, Mr. Moses descended with heavy steps, hand in hand with the day's hero and victim of canine disgrace, Olaf. When they got to the bottom, they parted ways. Mr. Moses took his mug behind the doorcurtains, sipping as he went, while the Viking took his place next to us in line without uttering a single unnecessary word. I looked at the clock. We'd been waiting for over ten minutes.

The front door slammed. The kid ran past us without stopping, leaping quietly up the stairs and leaving behind a smell of gasoline, sweat and perfume. I realized immediately that I could hear the voices of the owner and Kaisa in the kitchen, and a sort of strange suspicion dawned on me for the first time. I stared indecisively at the shower door.

"Have you been standing here a long time?" Olaf asked.

"Yes, quite a long time," Du Barnstoker said.

Suddenly, Hinkus muttered something unintelligible and, shoving Olaf's shoulder, rushed into the hall.

"Listen," I said. "Did anyone else arrive this morning?"

"Only these gentlemen," Du Barnstoker said. "Mr. Andvarafors and Mr. . . . um . . . the little fellow, who just left . . ."

Olaf objected. "We arrived last night," he said.

I already knew when they had arrived. For a second, the image of a skeleton purring out songs beneath the stream of hot water as it washed its armpits flashed across my mind. I lost my temper and shoved the door. It opened, of course. And of course, no one was in the shower. The stream of hot water (which had been left at full blast) was making a lot of noise, there was steam everywhere, the Dead Mountaineer's infamous tarpaulin jacket was hanging from the hook, and beneath this, on the oak bench, an old transistor radio was whispering and muttering.

"Que Diablo!" Du Barnstoker cried. "Where's the owner? Come here at once!"

A ruckus erupted. Heavy boots thumped as the owner ran to us. Simone emerged as if sprung from the ground. The kid leaned over the railing with a cigarette dangling from its lower lip. Hinkus watched cautiously from the hall.

"Unbelievable!" Du Barnstoker exclaimed heatedly. "We've been waiting and waiting, for no less than a quarter of an hour—isn't that right, Inspector?"

"And someone's been lying in my bed again," the child reported from above us. "And the towel's completely wet."

Simone's eyes flashed with impish glee.

"Gentlemen, gentlemen . . ." the owner said, offering a

series of appeasing gestures. Before doing anything else he
ducked into the shower and turned off the water. Then he took
the jacket off the hook, picked up the radio and turned to us.
His face was solemn. "Gentlemen!" he said in a low voice. "I
can only speak to the facts. This is HIS radio, gentlemen. And
HIS jacket."

"Exactly whose . . . ?" Olaf asked calmly.

"HIS. The dead mountaineer."

"What I meant was, whose turn is it exactly?" Olaf asked,
as calmly as before.

I silently maneuvered the owner out of the way, went into
the shower and locked the door behind me. After I'd already
taken my clothes off I realized that it wasn't my turn, but Simone's—but I didn't feel the slightest bit guilty. That was probably one of his, I thought furiously. Well, let him wait. The
hero of national science. What a waste of water . . . No, jokers
like him should be stopped. And punished. I'll teach you not
to play tricks on me . . .

When I left the shower, the people gathered in the hall
were still discussing what had happened. No new theories had
been offered, so I didn't stick around. On the stairs I ran into
the kid, who was still hanging over the railing.

"Madhouse!" it said to me defiantly. I passed without a
word and went straight to my room.

The shower and a pleasant exhausted feeling soon caused
my temper to disappear completely. I pulled the armchair up
to the window, picked up my fattest and most serious book
and sat down with my feet propped on the edge of the table.
Before I'd finished the first page, I was asleep; by the time I
woke up, maybe an hour and a half later, the sun had shifted
considerably, and the shadow of the inn was lying beneath
my window. I could tell from its silhouette that someone was
sitting on the roof, and I decided sleepily that this must be

Simone, the great physicist, hopping from chimney to chimney and chortling over the entire valley. I fell asleep again, waking finally with a start when my book slipped off onto the floor. Now I could distinctly see the shadows of two people on the roof: one appeared to be sitting, while the other was standing in front of him. Tanning, I thought, and went to wash up. While I was washing, it occurred to me that a cup of coffee might be nice, a good pick-me-up, and that a snack wouldn't be a bad thing either. I lit a cigarette and stepped into the hallway. It was already almost three.

I met Hinkus on the landing. He had just come down the attic stairs, and looked strange for some reason. He was naked to the waist and shiny with sweat; his face was so white it was practically green; his eyes weren't blinking; he was clutching a ball of crumpled clothes to his chest with both hands.

Catching sight of me, he shuddered visibly and stopped.

"Tanning?" I asked, out of politeness. "Don't get burned. You look ill."

Having expressed in this way concern for my fellow man's well-being, I walked past him downstairs without waiting for a response. Hinkus clonked his way down the stairs behind me.

"I need a drink," he said hoarsely.

"Hot up there?" I asked, without turning around.

"Y-yes . . . Very hot."

"Watch out," I said. "March sun in the mountains is a bad idea."

"I'm okay . . . I'll have a drink, and then I'll be okay."

We went down to the lobby.

"You should probably get dressed," I advised. "What if Mrs. Moses were there . . ."

"Right," he said. "Sure. I completely forgot."

He stopped and began hurriedly putting on his shirt and

jacket; I went down to the pantry, where I procured a plate of cold roast beef, some bread and coffee from Kaisa. Hinkus, dressed and looking much less green, joined me and demanded something stronger.

"Is Simone up there too?" I asked. The idea of whiling away some time with a game of pool had floated into my head.

"Up where?" Hinkus asked sharply, carefully bringing a full snifter to his lips.

"On the roof."

Hinkus's hand trembled, scattering drops of brandy on his palm. He took a quick gulp, stuck his nose into the air and, after wiping his mouth with his hand, said:

"No. No one else is up there."

I looked at him with surprise. His lips were pursed; he poured himself a second glass.

"That's strange," I said. "For some reason it seemed to me that Simone was up there with you—on the roof, I mean."

"Take a deep breath the next time anything 'seems' to you—you'll make fewer mistakes that way," the youth counselor replied, and drank. And then he poured himself another one.

"What's got into you?" I asked.

He stared at the full glass silently for a little while, before suddenly saying:

"Listen: do you want to suntan on the roof?"

"No thanks," I said. "I'm afraid of getting burned. Sensitive skin."

"You never go tanning?"

"No."

He thought about this, grabbed the bottle, screwed the cap back on.

"The air's great up there," he said. "And the view's gorgeous. The whole valley in the palm of your hand. The mountains . . ."

"Let's shoot some pool," I suggested. "Do you play?"

His sick little eyes looked me straight in the face for the first time.

"No," he said. "I'd rather get some fresh air."

He unscrewed the cap again and poured himself a fourth glass. I finished off my roast beef, drank my coffee and got up. Hinkus stared languidly into his brandy.

"Well, don't fall off the roof," I said.

He smiled curtly, but didn't respond. I went back up to the second floor again. I didn't hear any billiard balls clacking, so I made my way to Simone's room. No one answered my knock. Unintelligible voices were coming from behind the door to the next room, so I knocked on it. No Simone here, either. Du Barnstoker and Olaf were sitting at the table playing cards. In the middle of the table there was a tower of crumpled bills. When he saw me, Du Barnstoker made a sweeping gesture and exclaimed:

"Come in, come in, Inspector! My dear Olaf, you don't mind if the inspector sits in, do you?"

"Of course not," Olaf said, without looking up from his cards. "With pleasure." He called spades.

I apologized and closed the door. Where was that chortler hiding himself? I couldn't see, or more surprisingly hear him anywhere. And why did I even care?

I can shoot pool by myself. There's not much of a difference, really—I'd even say it's more fun. I set off for the billiard room; on the way there, I got a little shock. At the bottom of the attic stairs, pinching the hem of her long, luxurious dress with two fingers, was Mrs. Moses.

"Now you're tanning too?" I blurted out, unable to control myself.

"Tanning? Me? What an odd idea." She crossed the hall towards me. "What strange suggestions you make, Inspector!"

"Please don't call me Inspector," I asked. "I hear it enough on the job . . . To hear it now from you too . . ."

"I a-*dore* police officers," Mrs. Moses said, rolling her beautiful eyes. "They're heroes, men of courage . . . You're a brave man yourself, aren't you?"

Somehow it happened that I had offered her a hand and was leading her towards the billiard room. It was a white hand, hard and surprisingly cold.

"Madame," I said. "You're practically freezing . . ."

"Not at all, Inspector," she said, realizing her mistake at the last minute. "But then what can I call you now?"

"Peter, maybe?" I suggested.

"That would be charming. I had a friend named Peter once: Baron Von Gottesknecht. Perhaps you two know each other? . . . But then in that case, you must call me Olga. And what if Moses were to hear that?"

"He'll survive," I muttered. I glanced sideways at her extraordinary shoulders, her queenly neck, her proud profile, all of which made me hot to the point of chills. She's an idiot, I thought feverishly—but then so what? Whatever. A lot of people are idiots!

We passed through the dining room and found ourselves in the billiard room. Simone was there. For some reason he had pressed himself into a shallow but wide recess in the wall. His face was red and his hair disheveled.

"Simon!" shouted Mrs. Moses, putting her hands to her cheeks. "What on earth . . . ?"

In answer to this Simone let out a screech and, pushing his legs and arms against the sides of the recess, worked his way up to the ceiling.

"My god, you'll kill yourself!" Mrs. Moses cried.

"You know she's right, Simone," I said in annoyance. "Quit playing around or you'll break your neck."

The fool, however, was nowhere near breaking his neck and dying. He reached the ceiling, hung there for a second, growing even more flushed with blood, and then lightly and gently jumped to the floor, where he saluted us. Mrs. Moses began clapping.

"What a marvel you are, Simon," she said. "A human fly!"

"Well, Inspector?" said Simone, who was a little out of breath. "Shall we fight for the glory of this beautiful lady?" He picked up a cue and lunged towards me as if it were a fencing sword. "Inspector Glebsky, I challenge you to defend yourself!"

With these words he turned to the billiard table and, without taking time to aim, shot the eight ball across the table and into the corner pocket with such a crack that my eyes grew dark. However, retreat was out of the question. I gloomily picked up a cue.

"Fight, gentlemen, fight," Mrs. Moses said. "The beautiful woman will leave a token for the victor." She threw a lace handkerchief into the middle of the table. "But I have to go now. I'm afraid my Moses is already furious." She blew us her kisses and walked out.

"Devilishly attractive woman," Simone said. "Capable of driving a man out of his mind." He picked up the handkerchief with his cue, dipped his nose in its lace and rolled his eyes. "Charming! . . . I see you have also been unsuccessful in your attempts, Inspector?"

"Maybe if I spent as much time around her as you do," I said darkly, gathering the balls into the rack. "Who asked you to hang around here in the billiard room, anyway?"

"You didn't have to bring her here, blockhead," Simone rejoined reasonably.

"Well, I couldn't take her to my room," I snapped.

"You shouldn't start things you don't know how to finish,"

Simone advised. "And rack the balls more evenly, you're playing with an expert here . . . There. What shall we play? London
Bridge?"

"No. Something simpler."

"Something simpler," Simone agreed.

He placed the handkerchief carefully on the windowsill,
paused for a second, lowered his head and peered through the
window at something. Then he returned to the table.

"Do you remember what Hannibal did to the Romans near
Cannes?"

"All right, all right," I said. "Let's get going."

"I'll jog your memory," Simone said. With a series of elegant movements he nudged the cueball out to where he
wanted it with his cue, took aim, and sunk it. Then he sunk
another ball, and split the pyramid. Then, without giving me
time to take any of his victims out of their pockets, he sunk
two balls in a row, before finally whiffing.

"Lucky for you," he said, chalking his cue. "Now let's see
what you can do."

I walked around the table, picking off the easiest ball.

"Look," Simone said. He was again standing at the window
and looking out at something off to one side. "Some fool is
sitting on the roof . . . Excuse me—*two* fools! I mistook the
standing one for a chimney. It appears that my triumphs have
spawned imitators."

"That's Hinkus," I muttered, trying to get in a better position for my shot.

"Hinkus—that's the little one who's always whining,"
said Simone. "A scrap. Olaf on the other hand. The descendent of the ancient Scandinavian kings, believe me, Inspector
Glebsky."

Finally, I took my shot. And missed. It was a simple shot,
too. Too bad. I stared at the end of the cue, examining its pad.

"There's nothing to see—nothing at all," Simone said, approaching the table. "You've got no excuse."

"What's your shot?" I asked, watching him in confusion.

"Two sides and then the middle," he said with an innocent look.

I groaned and went to stand by the window, in order not to see. Simone shot. Then he shot again. Snap, crack, pop. Then he shot again and said:

"Sorry, Inspector. Proceed."

The shadow of the seated man threw his head back and raised a hand with a bottle in it. I saw that it was Hinkus. He'll swallow and then pass the bottle to the standing figure. But who was standing?

"Are you going to shoot or not?" Simone asked. "What is it?"

"Hinkus is getting drunk," I said. "Today's the day he falls off the roof."

Hinkus took a deep swig and then took up his previous pose. He didn't pass the bottle. Who was standing anyway? The kid, probably . . . Interesting, what could the kid have to talk to Hinkus about? I returned to the table, chose the easier ball and missed again.

"Have you read Coriolis's memoir on billiards?" Simone asked.

"No," I said gloomily. "And I don't plan to."

"Well, I have," Simone said. He finished me off with two shots and broke at last into his creepy giggle. I lay my cue across the table.

"There's no one left to play with, Simone," I said bitterly. "I guess now you can blow your nose in your prize by yourself."

Simone grabbed the handkerchief and solemnly tucked it into his breast pocket.

"Excellent," he said. "What shall we do now?"

I thought about this.

"I think I'll have a shave. It's almost lunch."

"What about me?" Simone asked.

"You can play some pool with yourself," I advised. "Or go to Olaf's room. Do you have any money? If you do, they'll greet you with open arms."

"Ah," Simone said. "I've already been there."

"What—already?"

"I lost two hundred crowns to Olaf. He plays like a machine—not a single mistake. It's not even interesting. I set Barnstoker on him. He's a magician, after all, maybe he can pull a card trick on him . . ."

We went out into the hallway and immediately bumped into the child of Du Barnstoker's beloved deceased brother. The kid stood in our way, its black bulging goggles gleaming brazenly at us. It asked for a cigarette.

"How was Hinkus?" I asked, pulling out a pack. "Is he totally soused?"

"Hinkus? Um . . ." The kid lit the cigarette and, curling its lips into a circle, puffed out some smoke. "Not totally, but he kicked the first bottle and started on another one."

"Oho," I said. "On his second already . . ."

"What else is there to do here?" the kid asked.

"Were you drinking with him?" Simone asked with interest. The kid snorted haughtily.

"Not likely! He barely noticed me. After all, Kaisa was there . . ."

It occurred to me that here was an opportunity to figure out definitively whether I was talking to a boy or a girl. So I laid my trap.

"You were in the pantry then?" I said insinuatingly.

"Yes. So what? The police don't allow that?"

"The police just want to know what you were doing there."

"The scientific community, too," Simone added. It appeared that we'd had the same idea.

"Do I need a permit to drink coffee?" the child inquired.

"No," I answered. "And what else were you doing there?"

Now she'll . . . that is to say, *it* will say something like, "I had a nibble," or "I wolfed down two sandwiches."

"Nothing," the child said coolly. "Coffee and pastries with cream. That's all that happened in the pantry."

"Sweets before dinner aren't good for you," Simone said reproachfully. He was clearly disappointed. I was too.

"As for getting drunk in the middle of the day: that's not my cup of tea," the kid concluded victoriously. "I'll leave that to Hinkus."

"Fair enough," I muttered. "I'm going to go shave."

"Any more questions, officer?" the kid called after us.

"No. Peace be with you," I said.

The door slammed—the kid had retired to its room.

"I think I'll have a little bite to eat," Simone said, lingering on the landing. "Come on, Inspector—there's still an hour before lunch . . ."

"I know what kind of a bite you're looking for," I said. "Go on, I'm a family man, Kaisa doesn't interest me."

Simone chuckled and said, "If you're such a family man, can you tell me, was that a boy or a girl? I'm stumped."

"Go play with Kaisa," I said. "Leave the puzzles to the police . . . By the way, were you the one who pulled that prank with the shower?"

"I wouldn't have dreamed of it," Simone said. "If you want to know, in my opinion, it was the owner himself."

I shrugged, and we went our separate ways. Simone's boots pounded up the stairs as I headed for my room. The moment that I passed the door to the museum, I heard a crash, something toppled with a roar, there was the sound of glass breaking and frustrated grumbling. Without a second's hesitation, I tore the door open and flew into the room, practically knocking Mr. Moses off his feet. Mr. Moses, who was lifting a corner of the carpet up with one hand, and in the other clutching his perennial mug, was looking with disgust at the overturned nightstand and the pieces of broken vase.

"Blasted rattrap," he croaked at the sight of me. "Filthy den."

"What are you doing in here?" I asked angrily.

Mr. Moses immediately lost his temper.

"What am I doing here?" he bellowed, jerking the carpet up with all his strength. Doing this, he nearly lost his balance and knocked over a chair. "Here I am, searching for the scoundrel who's been tottering around our inn, stealing things from decent people, stomping up and down the hallway every night and staring through the window at my wife! Why the devil should I have to do this, when there's an officer of the law on the premises?"

He threw the rug back down and turned to me. I took a step back.

"Maybe I should offer a reward?" he continued, working himself up. "The damned police don't lift a finger until there's a reward involved. All right—how much do you want, Inspector? Five hundred? A thousand? Very well: fifteen hundred crowns to the man who finds my missing gold watch! Two thousand crowns!"

"You lost your watch?" I asked, frowning.

"Yes!"

"When did you notice it was missing?"

"Only a second ago!"

The jokes were over. A gold watch: that wasn't felt slippers or a showering ghost.

"When did you last see the item in question?"

"Early this morning."

"Where do you usually keep it?"

"I do not keep watches—I use them! It was lying on my desk!"

I thought this over.

"My advice," I said finally, "is for you to write out a formal statement. Then I'll call the police."

Moses stared at me, and for a few minutes neither of us said anything. Then he took a sip from his mug and said, "To hell with your formal statement and the police. The last thing I want is for my name to fall into the hands of some grubby newspaper reporter. Why can't you get to work on it yourself? I said I'd offer a reward. Do you want an advance?"

"I'm not comfortable intervening in this case," I said, shrugging my shoulders. "I'm a civil servant, not a private detective. There's professional procedure to be considered, and anyway . . ."

"All right," he said suddenly. "I'll think about it . . ." He paused. "Maybe it will turn up. Hopefully, it was all just another idiotic joke. But if the watch isn't found by tomorrow morning, I'll write your statement."

We all agreed that this would be best. Moses went his way, and I went mine.

Who knows what new clues Moses found in his room. I had plenty of them in mine. For starters, someone had hung a sign on my door that said: "When I hear the word 'culture,' I call the police." I took it down, of course—but that was just the beginning. The table in my room appeared to be covered in hardened gum Arabic. Someone had poured it out of the bottle, which was lying in plain sight. In the center of the dried puddle was a piece of paper. A note. An utterly ridiculous note. In clumsy block letters: "MISTER INSPECTOR GLEBSKY: PLEASE BE INFORMED THAT A DANGEROUS GANGSTER, SADIST

AND MANIAC IS CURRENTLY STAYING AT THE INN UNDER THE NAME HINKUS. IN CRIMINAL CIRCLES, HE GOES BY THE NAME 'THE FINCH'. HE IS ARMED AND THREATENING DEATH TO ONE OF THE INN'S CLIENTS. MISTER INSPECTOR IS KINDLY REQUESTED TO TAKE SOME SORT OF ACTION."

I was so furious and dumbfounded by this that I had to read the note twice before I understood what it said. When I was finished I lit a cigarette and looked around the room. Naturally, I didn't find any footprints. I smoothed out the sign I'd crumpled up and compared it to the note. The letters on the sign were also in block print and clumsily written, but they'd been written with a pencil. Anyway, the business with the sign was clear: it had to be the kid's work. A simple joke. One of those stupid signs that the French scrawled on their Sorbonne. The note was something different, however. A practical joker might have slipped it under the door, or stuck it in the lock, or just left it on the table under something heavy, like an ashtray. You had to be either a complete cretin or a savage to ruin a perfectly good table for the sake of a stupid prank. I read the note again, took the deepest drag I could and then went to the window. There goes my vacation, I thought. There goes that freedom I've been waiting so long for . . .

The sun was already quite low in the sky, the shadow of the inn stretched out a good hundred meters. Mr. Hinkus, the dangerous gangster, maniac and sadist, was still loitering on the roof. He was alone.

5.

I stopped in front of Hinkus's room and looked around carefully. The hallway was empty, as usual. A sound of clicking balls was coming from the billiard room—that was Simone. Du Barnstoker was still fleecing Olaf in Olaf's room. The kid was occupied with its motorcycle. The Moseses were in their room. Hinkus was sitting on the roof. Five minutes ago he had gone down to the pantry, grabbed another bottle, gone into his room, put on his fur coat, and now apparently intended to continue taking in the fresh air at least until lunchtime. As for me, I was standing in front of his room, trying key after key from the ring that I'd swiped from the owner's office, and preparing to commit a misdemeanor. Without a warrant I obviously had no right to break into someone else's room and perform a search there or even a quick inspection. But I felt that it was necessary, otherwise my sleep and even peace of mind could be at stake.

The fifth or sixth key clicked softly, and I slipped into the room. I did this just like a hero in a spy thriller would have—I didn't know how else to do it. The sun had almost gone behind the ridge, but it was light enough in the room. It appeared unoccupied: the bed was barely ruffled, the ashtray was empty and clean, and both of the trunks were standing right in the middle of the room. It was impossible to imagine that someone was intending to stay here for two weeks.

The contents of the first and heavier trunk only increased my apprehension. It was your typical decoy bag: some rags, torn sheets and pillowcases and a bunch of books that had clearly been selected at random. Hinkus had obviously stuffed this trunk with whatever was at hand. The real luggage was in the second trunk. Here I found three changes of underwear, a pair of pajamas, a cosmetics bag, a bundle of money—a big bundle, bigger than the one I'd brought with me—and two dozen handkerchiefs. There was also a small silver flask (empty), a box with sunglasses and a bottle with a foreign label on it (full). And at the very bottom of the trunk, beneath the underwear, a massive gold watch with an intricate face, and a small woman's Browning.

I sat on the floor, listening. Right now everything was quiet, but I knew I didn't have much time to think. I examined the watch. An elaborate monogram of some kind had been engraved on the lid. It was real gold, pure, with a reddish sheen; the dial was decorated with the signs of the zodiac. There was no doubt about it: it was Mr. Moses's watch. I turned my attention to the pistol. A pretty little toy, pearl-handled and with a .25 caliber nickel-plated barrel: a weapon for close quarters, to be frank not much of a weapon at all . . . Nonsense: it was all nonsense. Gangsters don't waste time on trinkets like these. For that matter, gangsters don't steal watches, even ones as big and old as this—real gangsters, I mean, with names and reputations. Especially in an inn, on their first day there, where they could be caught red-handed.

All right, then, let's review the case. There was no evidence that Hinkus was a dangerous gangster, maniac and sadist, and plenty that someone wanted me to think of him that way. True, there was the false luggage . . . Okay, I'll deal with that later.

What about the pistol and watch? If I take them, and Hinkus really is the thief (though not a gangster), then he'll get away with it . . . If they've been planted . . . Damn, I can't figure it out . . . Not enough experience. I'm not Hercule Poirot . . . If I take them, then where am I supposed to put them? Carry them on me? I might be accused of stealing them . . . And I can't hide them in my room . . .

I listened, again. I could hear utensils clicking in the dining room—Kaisa was setting the tables. Someone stomped past the door. Simone's voice asked loudly: "But where's the inspector? Where's our White Knight?" Kaisa screeched sharply, chilly laughter shook the floorboards. It was time to make my getaway.

I couldn't think of anything else to do, so I hurriedly emptied the clip, put the cartridges in my pocket, and returned the pistol and the watch to the bottom of the trunk. I had barely managed to sneak out and turn the key behind me when Du Barnstoker appeared at the other end of the hall. Turning his aristocratic profile towards me, he spoke to someone—Olaf, it looked like.

"My dear fellow, what's there to talk about? When has a Du Barnstoker ever refused a rematch? Let it be tonight, if you wish! Ten o'clock, say, in your room . . ."

I tried to look casual (in other words, I took out a toothpick and began using it). Catching sight of me, Du Barnstoker gave a friendly wave.

"My dear inspector!" he shouted. "Victory, glory, riches! These are the Du Barnstokers' dues!"

I walked towards him, and we met outside the door to his room.

"You cleaned out Olaf?"

"Imagine that!" he said, smiling happily. "Our dear Olaf is too methodical, he plays like a machine, no imagination.

Boring, even . . . Hold on a second—what do we have here?"
He reached deftly into my breast pocket and removed a
playing card. "The same ace that I used to finish off poor
Olaf . . ."

Poor Olaf came out of his room looking huge, rosy, light
on his feet; he smiled good-naturedly as he passed us, and
muttered, "A drink before dinner . . ." Du Barnstoker, smiling,
followed him with his eyes and then grabbed me by the sleeve
suddenly, as if he'd just remembered something.

"By the way, my dear inspector, do you know what new
joke our dear departed friend has pulled on us? Come to my
room for just a second . . ."

He pulled me into his room, shoved me into a chair and
offered me a cigar.

"Where has it gone?" he muttered, patting his pockets.
"Aha! Here, have a look at what I received today." He handed
me a crumpled piece of paper.

Another note. Written in clumsy block letters, with gram-
matical mistakes: "WE FOUND YOU. I GOTS YOU AT
GUNPOINT. DONT TRY TO ESCAPE OR DO ANYTHING
STUPID. I WILL SHOOT WITHOUT WARNINGS. F."

Gritting my cigar between my teeth, I read through the
message twice and then once more.

"Charming, no?" Du Barnstoker said, pouting at himself
in the mirror. "It's even signed. We should ask the manager
what the Dead Mountaineer's name was . . ."

"Where did this come from?"

"It was delivered to Olaf's room while we were playing.
Olaf went to the pantry to get a drink, and I sat and smoked a
cigar. There was a knock at the door, I said, 'Yes, yes, come in,'
but no one came in. I was surprised, and suddenly I saw that
there was a note on the floor. Apparently someone had slipped
it under the door."

"Of course you looked out into the hallway, and of course you didn't see anyone," I said.

"Well, it took me quite some time to pry myself out of the chair," Du Barnstoker said. "Shall we? To be honest, I'm ravenously hungry."

I put the note in my pocket, and we made our way to the dining room, having picked up the kid along the way, though without succeeding in persuading it to wash its hands.

"You have a sort of worried look about you, Inspector," Du Barnstoker remarked, when we'd gotten to the dining room.

Looking into his bright old eyes, it occurred to me suddenly that he was behind this entire story about the notes. For a second I was seized by a cold fury; I wanted to stamp my feet and scream: "Leave me alone! Let me ski in peace and quiet!" But of course, I kept a hold on myself.

We entered the dining room. Apparently everyone was already there. Mrs. Moses was serving Mr. Moses, Simone and Olaf were puttering around the appetizers, the manager was pouring the liqueur. Du Barnstoker and the kid headed for their usual place at the table, and I joined the other men. Simone was lecturing Olaf, in an evil-sounding whisper, on the effects that edelweiss liqueur had on the human organs. He listed them: leukemia, jaundice, duodenal cancer. Olaf hemmed and hawed good-naturedly as he ate his caviar. Then Kaisa came in and proceeded to prattle away to the owner:

"He doesn't want to go, he says if we're not all here, then he won't show up. And when everyone shows up, he'll come too. That's what he said . . . Two empty bottles . . ."

"So then go and tell him that everyone's here already," the owner told her.

"He won't believe me, I told him that already, that everyone's here, and he . . ."

"Who are we talking about?" Mr. Moses asked abruptly.

"We're talking about Mr. Hinkus," the owner responded. "He's still on the roof, and I would like . . ."

"What do you mean 'on the roof'?" the kid said in a husky bass. "He's right there—Hinkus!" It thrust a fork with a pickle on it at Olaf.

"My child, you are mistaken," Du Barnstoker said softly, as Olaf offered a friendly grin and boomed, "Olaf Andvarafors, at your service, little one. You can call me Olaf."

"Well, then what does he . . . ?" The child thrust the pickle and fork in my direction.

"Gentlemen, gentlemen!" the owner said. "There's no need to argue. All of this is simple foolishness. Mr. Hinkus is taking advantage of a freedom that we allow all our guests—to be up on the roof—and Kaisa is now going to bring him down here."

"But he won't come . . ."

"What the devil, Snevar!" Moses said. "If he doesn't want to come down, then let him freeze up there."

"My esteemed Mr. Moses," the manager said with dignity, "It is my deepest wish that we all be together at this point. I have some very good news to announce to my esteemed guests. Kaisa, quickly!"

"But he won't come . . ."

I set my plate of appetizers on the table.

"Hold on a second," I said. "I'll get him."

As I left the room I heard Simone say, "Excellent! Let the police do their job, finally," and then burst into spooky laughter, which followed me up the attic stairs.

I climbed the stairs, pushed open an unfinished wooden door and found myself in a sort of circular pavilion with windows all around and narrow benches for resting lining the walls. It was cold in here, with a strange smell of snow and dust; there was a mountain of stacked deck chairs. A plywood door, leading outside, had been left ajar.

The flat roof was covered with a thick layer of snow, which was packed hard around the pavilion; further along there was a walkway leading out to the inn's crooked radio antenna. At the end of this walkway, a fur-coated Hinkus was sitting silently in a deck chair. His left hand held a bottle on his knee; his right was hidden against his chest, no doubt to keep it warm. His face was barely even visible, it was covered by his coat collar and the brim of his fur hat, from between which his watchful eyes shone out like a tarantula peering out of its burrow.

"Come on, Hinkus," I said. "Everyone's down there."

"Everyone?" he asked hoarsely.

I exhaled a puff of steam, walked closer and stuffed my hands in my pockets.

"Every single one. We're waiting for you."

"So, everyone . . ." Hinkus repeated.

I nodded and looked around. The sun had hidden itself behind the ridge, the snow in the valley looked purple, in the dark sky a pale moon was rising.

Out of the corner of my eye I noticed that Hinkus was watching me closely.

"Well, why wait for me?" he said. "They should have just started . . . Why all the fuss?"

"The owner has some sort of surprise, and he needs all of us together."

"A surprise," Hinkus said, and coughed. "I've got tuberculosis," he said suddenly. "The doctors say I need to spend as much time as possible in the fresh air . . . And eat chicken. Dark meat," he added, after a second of silence.

I was starting to feel sorry for him.

"That's too bad. Damn," I said. "But all the same, you need to eat . . ."

"Of course," he said and stood up. "I'll eat some dinner and then come back out here." He placed the bottle in the snow. "Do you think the doctors are lying? I mean, as far as the fresh air goes . . ."

"I don't think so," I said. I remembered how pale and greenish he'd looked when he came downstairs that afternoon, and asked, "Listen, why are you drinking so much vodka? It can't be good for you."

"Oooh!" he said, in quiet desperation. "How am I supposed to make it without vodka?" He was silent. We went downstairs. "Without vodka, I wouldn't have anything," he said resolutely. "It would be terrible. I'd go out of my mind without vodka."

"There there, Hinkus," I said. "Tuberculosis is treatable now. This isn't the nineteenth century."

"You're right," he agreed slowly. We turned down the hallway. In the dining room, dishes were ringing out, voices were humming. "Go on ahead, I'm going to get rid of my fur coat," he said, stopping outside his door.

I nodded and went into the dining room.

"Where's the suspect?" Simone asked loudly.

"I told you he wouldn't come," Kaisa squealed.

"Everything's fine," I said. "He's coming."

I sat in my old place; then, remembering the way things went here, I got up and went to get soup. Du Barnstoker was talking about magic numbers. Mrs. Moses was gasping. Simone laughed abruptly. "Bardel, Dubert, stop this . . ." Mr. Moses grumbled. "Medieval nonsense, all of it." I was pouring myself some soup when Hinkus appeared in the dining room. His lips were trembling, and he looked green again for some reason. He was greeted by an explosion of cheers, but he hastily looked around the table, making his way uncertainly to his place between me and Olaf.

"No, no, no!" the owner cried, running up to him with a glass of liqueur in hand. "Baptism by fire!"

Hinkus stopped, looked at the glass and said something that I couldn't hear over the noise.

"No, no, no!" the owner said. "This is the best medicine. The cure for all your sorrows! A panacea, in other words. Please!"

Hinkus didn't argue. He poured the liquid into his mouth, put the glass on the tray and took his seat at the table.

"Now there's a man!" Mrs. Moses called out admiringly. "Gentlemen: here is a true specimen!"

I went back to my place and proceeded to tuck in. Hinkus hadn't gotten any soup, he'd only taken a little bit of the roast. He didn't look so bad now—he seemed to be thinking intensely about something. I had just started listening to Du Barnstoker's rant when the manager clinked a knife against his plate.

"Ladies and gentlemen!" he called out solemnly. "If I could ask for a moment of your attention! Now that we are all gathered here together, I will allow myself the pleasure of giving you some good news. In response to overwhelming requests from the guests, the inn's administration has decided to hold a gala ball tonight, in honor of the Beginning of Spring. Tonight's dinner will not end! Dancing, ladies and gentlemen, wine, cards, pleasant conversation!"

Simone clapped his bony hands together with a bang. Mrs. Moses started clapping too. Everyone perked up, and even the stone-faced Mr. Moses, after taking a hard swallow from his mug, hissed, "Well, then, cards are all right . . ." The kid drummed a fork against the table and stuck its tongue out at me. A pink tongue, very pleasant-looking. And then, at the very height of this tumult and excitement, Hinkus suddenly leaned towards me and whispered in my ear:

"Listen, Inspector, you're a policeman . . . What should

I do? I wanted to take something out of my trunk . . . some medicine. They told me to drink it before dinner . . . And I had . . . well . . . some warm clothes, a fur vest, socks . . . None of my stuff was in there. There were just some rags—not my own, torn-up underwear, some books . . ."

I carefully laid my spoon on the table and looked at him. His eyes were circles, full of fear, and his right eyelid was twitching. A head gangster. A maniac and a sadist.

"All right," I said through my teeth. "What do you want me to do about it?"

He immediately shrunk somehow, pulling his head back into his shoulders.

"Oh no . . . nothing . . . Only I didn't know whether it was a joke or . . . After all, if someone stole something, you're a policeman—aren't you? . . . It's got to be a joke, don't you think?"

"Yes, Hinkus," I said, lowering my eyes and again turning my attention to the soup. "They're all jokers here, you know that. Think of it as a joke, Hinkus."

6.

To my great surprise, the party turned out to be a success. Everyone stuck around after hurrying through their meals— everyone, that is, except for Hinkus, who muttered some excuses and stomped back up to the roof to continue bathing his lungs in the mountain air. I felt a little sorry for him as I watched him go. I even thought for a second about heading back to his room and taking that damned watch out of his trunk. A joke's a joke, but he could get into serious trouble. He's got enough problems already, I thought. I was tired of these worries, tired of these jokes, tired of my own stupidity . . . I'm going to get drunk, I decided, and instantly felt better. I exchanged my shot glass for a tumbler, and looked quickly around the table. What did any of this have to do with me? I was on vacation. And anyway, I'm not a policeman. Who cares how I'd signed in . . . If you want to know, I'm actually a salesman. I sell secondhand sinks. Toilets too . . . It occurred to me that for a counselor, even a youth counselor, Hinkus had a pretty poor vocabulary. I shook this thought out of my head and cackled diligently over some clumsy witticism of Simone's that I hadn't heard. I swallowed a half glass of brandy in a single gulp and poured myself another one. My head started to buzz.

Meanwhile, the fun was starting. Kaisa hadn't had a chance

to clear the dirty dishes yet; meanwhile, after communicating their intentions to one another via a series of hospitable gestures, Mr. Moses and Du Barnstoker moved to the green cloth-covered card table that had appeared suddenly in a corner of the dining room. The owner put on some loud music. Olaf and Simone approached Mrs. Moses simultaneously, and, since she was unable to choose between her two cavaliers, the three of them proceeded to dance together. The kid showed me its tongue again. Well, all right, then! I got up from the table and stumbled my way towards this hooligan, this bandit. It was now or never, I thought. Anyway, this kind of investigation was more interesting than stolen watches and other junk. But I'm a salesman. Of well- and even miraculously preserved sinks . . .

"May I have this dance, Mademoiselle?" I asked, plunking myself down on the seat next to the kid.

"Madame, I don't dance," the kid answered lazily. "Now shut up and give me a cigarette."

I gave him a cigarette, glugged some more brandy and proceeded to explain to this creature that his behavior—his be-ha-vi-or—was unconscionable, and had to stop. That I'd whip him if he didn't watch it. Or write him up, I added after thinking it over for a few seconds, for the public exhibition of improper attire. Also writing slogans, I said. That's no good. On doors. Shocking and rebellious behavior—rebellious! I'm an honest salesman, and I won't let anyone . . . A brilliant thought occurred to me . . . I'll complain to the police about you, I said, bursting into a giddy laugh. And may I suggest this . . . no, not a toilet, that would be unseemly, especially at the dinner table . . . but how about a beautiful sink? Miraculously preserved, in spite of everything. It's a *Pavel Bure*. What do you think? Treat yourself!

The kid answered me, ingeniously, first in a boy's husky

bass, then in a gentle girlish alto. My head began to spin; it was starting to feel like I was having a conversation with two people. On the one hand, there was this spoiled teenager who'd gone to seed, who continually stole my brandy, and to whom I had responsibilities as a member of the police force, an experienced salesperson, and a person of higher rank. On the other, there was that charming and piquant girl, who was nothing like my old lady (thank god), and towards whom I was apparently starting to feel more than just paternal feelings. Shoving aside the teenager, who kept trying to butt in on our conversation, I told the girl my definition of marriage as the voluntary union of two hearts that have taken on certain moral obligations. And no bicycles or motorcycles, I added sternly. Let's agree to that up front. My old lady can't stand such things . . . We agreed and drank, me and the teenager first, then me and the girl, my bride. Why in god's name shouldn't a girl, who was of age mind you, have a little good brandy? Having repeated this question three times (not without some slight belligerence), I leaned back in my chair and looked around the room.

Everything was going swimmingly. No laws were being broken, no moral statutes violated. No one was posting slogans, writing notes, or stealing watches. The music was thundering along. Du Barnstoker, Moses and the owner were playing Thirteen, with no limit on the pot size. Mrs. Moses was dancing daringly with Simone to some very modern music, Kaisa was clearing our plates. She was surrounded, by dishes, forks, Olafs. All of the dishes on the table were in motion—I barely managed to grab a passing bottle and spill it on my pants.

"Brun, buddy," I said earnestly, "Don't give it another thought. It's all just a big joke. Gold watches, dust covers . . ." Here I was struck by a new thought. "Let me ask you something," I said, "What would you say to friendly shooting lesson?"

"I'm not your buddy," the girl said sadly. "I'm your bride."

"All the better," I shouted enthusiastically. "I have a ladies' Browning . . ."

We talked for a while about guns, wedding rings, and, for some reason, telekinesis. I began to feel more reluctant.

"No!" I said, decisively. "I disagree. First, take your glasses off. I want to know what I'm getting here."

This was a mistake. The offended girl disappeared off somewhere, leaving me with the teenager, who started being rude. But just at that moment Mrs. Moses came up and asked me to dance, which I did gladly. A minute later, I'd decided that I'd been an idiot: that my fate lay with Mrs. Moses, and with her alone. With my Olga. Her immaculately soft hands weren't in the least bit chapped or cut, and she willingly allowed me to kiss them; she also had beautiful, distinctly visible eyes, which weren't hidden by goggles; a pleasant smell clung to her; plus she wasn't the sister of a rough and impudent youth who wouldn't let you get a word in edgewise. True, Simone seemed to be constantly circling her (the great physicist, the dull fool) but one could learn how to get used to that, since the two of them weren't related. We were grown-ups, after all; we indulged in sensual pleasures on our doctors' advice, and, when we stepped on one another's feet, we admitted it in an honorable and manly way: "Pardon me, old man, my mistake . . ."

At a certain point I found myself completely sober and standing behind the window-curtain with Mrs. Moses. I was holding her around the waist, as she rested her head on my shoulder, saying, "Oh darling, what a lovely view! . . ."

The unexpected informality of her address embarrassed me, and I stared dumbly out the window, thinking all the while about how I might delicately remove my hand from her waist before we were caught. The view really was quite nice. The moon must have already been quite high; the whole valley looked blue under its light, and the nearby mountains appeared to be hanging in the still air. Then I noticed the gray shadow of unhappy Hinkus doubled up on the roof, and muttered, "Poor Hinkus . . ."

Mrs. Moses pulled away gently and stared up at me.

"Poor?" she asked. "Why poor?"

"He's sick," I explained. "He has tuberculosis, and he's very scared."

"Of course," she nodded. "You've noticed it too? He seems to always be scared. A suspicious and quite unpleasant individual—hardly one of ours . . ."

I shook my head heavily and sighed.

"There you go again," I said. "But there's nothing to be suspicious of—he's just a sad and lonely man. Very pathetic. You should have seen how he turned green and started sweating . . . And then there are all the jokes everyone's playing on him . . ."

Suddenly she laughed her charming crystalline laugh.

"Count Greystock was the same way—constantly turning green. It was quite amusing!"

I didn't know what to say; removing my hand with relief, finally, from her waist, I offered her a cigarette. She declined and began talking about counts, barons, viscounts and princes. Watching her speak, I tried to remember why on earth I'd gone behind the curtain.

Then the curtain parted with a rustle and there was the kid. Without looking at me, it shuffled its feet awkwardly and in a choked voice said, "*Permette vous . . .*"

"*Bitte*, dear boy," Mrs. Moses said, flashing me another dazzling smile as she glided over the parquet in the kid's arms.

I exhaled and wiped my forehead with a handkerchief. The table had been cleared by now. The trio of card players continued to deal in the corner. Simone was thrashing away at the billiard balls. Olaf and Kaisa had evaporated. The music was rumbling at half volume, Mrs. Moses and Brun were demonstrating their remarkable skill. I walked carefully past them and into the billiard room.

Simone greeted me with a wave of his cue; without wasting a precious second he offered me a five-ball handicap. I took off my jacket, rolled up my sleeves, and we began. I lost a large number of games, for which I was punished with a large number of jokes. My mood began to improve significantly. I laughed at his jokes, which I didn't quite understand, since they concerned things like quarks and Schrödinger cats and professors with exotic names; I drank my club soda, paying no attention to the mockery and entreaties of my partner; I moaned dramatically and clutched at my heart when I blundered, acted out my immoderate delight when I scored; I thought up new rules and defended them heatedly—I let myself go so thoroughly that at one point I took off my tie and unbuttoned my collar. I was in fine feather, in my opinion. Simone was too. He made shots at incredible, theoretically impossible angles; he ran around the walls and even, it seemed, along the ceiling; in the pauses between jokes he sang songs about mathematical theories at the top of his voice; he addressed me informally over and over again, and then corrected himself with a "My apologies, old man. It's this damned democratic education . . . !"

Through the billiard room's open door I briefly glimpsed Olaf dancing with the kid, then the owner carrying a tray of drinks to the card players, then a flushed Kaisa. The music blasted, the card players screamed with excitement, laying down spades, collecting hearts, trumping diamonds. Every

once in a while a hoarse voice could be heard: "Listen, Drab-
ble . . . Bandrel . . . Du . . . !" and the mad knock of a mug
against the table, and the owner's voice, "Gentlemen, gentlemen! What is money but so much ash . . . ?" and the ringing
crystal laughter of Mrs. Moses, "Moses, what are you doing,
the spades have been gobbled up already . . ." Then the clocks
struck something-thirty, the chairs were being moved in the
dining room, and I saw Moses slap Du Barnstoker on the back
with his mug-free hand, and growl, "As you wish, gentlemen,
but it's time for the Moseses to get some sleep. A good game,
Barny . . . Barnbell . . . you, you're a crafty adversary. Gentlemen, goodnight! Come, my love . . ." I remember Simone saying he was out of gas, as he put it. I went into the dining hall
for a new bottle of brandy, having decided that it was time for
me to replenish my stores of fun and lightheartedness.

The music was still playing but the hall was already empty,
except for Du Barnstoker, who was sitting at the card table
with his back to me, pensively performing card tricks with
a pair of decks. With smooth movements of his slim white
fingers, he plucked cards out of the air, made them van-
ish from his outstretched palms, blew a fan of shimmer-
ing cards from one hand into the other, scattered the entire
deck into the air in front of him and then sent it to oblivion.
He hadn't noticed me, and I wasn't going to distract him. I
took a bottle from the bar and tiptoed back into the billiard
room.

When the bottle was a little less than halfway gone, I took
a shot so strong that it caused two balls to jump off the table at
the same time, and tore the billiard cloth. Simone was moved
to admiration, but I decided I'd had enough.

"That's it," I said, setting down my cue. "I need some
fresh air."

I crossed the now-empty dining room, made my way

down the hall and went out onto the porch. For some reason I felt sad that the party had come to an end without anything interesting happening; that I had wasted my chance with Mrs. Moses and, if memory served, rattled off some nonsense to the child of Du Barnstoker's late brother; that the moon was bright, tiny and icy-looking; and that around me for many miles there was nothing but snow and rocks. I had a talk with the St. Bernard, who was making his nightly rounds; he agreed that the night was too quiet and empty, and that solitude, despite its numerous benefits, was really a lousy thing. Still, he refused outright to break the valley's silence and join me in a howl, or even just a good bark. In response to my request he just shook his head, walked away with a dissatisfied look and lay down by the porch.

I walked back and forth on the clear path in front of the inn, gazing up at the façade, which was bathed in blue moonlight. The kitchen window was glowing yellow, Mrs. Moses's bedroom window was rose-colored, there was another light coming from Du Barnstoker's room, and behind the curtains in the dining room; all the other windows were dark, including Olaf's, which was wide open, as it had been that morning. On the roof, Hinkus the martyr protruded, bundled to his ears in a fur coat, looking as lonely as Lel and I but even less happy under his burden of illness and fear.

"Hinkus!" I called quietly, but he didn't move. Maybe he was sleeping, or maybe he didn't hear me through the heavy earmuffs and turned-up collar.

I was freezing, but I felt cheered up by the fact that it was now time to avail myself of a fine old hotel tradition, and drink some hot port.

"Come on, Lel," I said, and we went back into the hall. There we met the owner, and I let him in on my plan. We were in total sympathy with one another.

"Now is the perfect time for sitting in front of the fireplace," he said. "Go on ahead, Peter, please—I'll get things ready."

I accepted his invitation and, after grabbing a place by the fire, began warming my freezing hands. I listened as the owner walked down the hall, muttered something to Kaisa and then kept walking, flipping switches as he went. His footsteps grew quieter, and the music in the dining room shut off. He plodded heavily down the stairs and then walked back up the hall again, lecturing Lel softly. "No, Lel, don't pester me," he said sternly. "You've disgraced yourself again—in the house this time. Mr. Olaf complained to me. What a shame. Where have you ever seen a respectable dog do something like that?"

So, the Viking had suffered a second embarrassment, I thought with no small amount of relish. My gloating increased as I recalled how avidly Olaf had danced in the dining room with the kid. When Lel approached me with his head bowed in shame, and nudged his cold nose into my fist, I patted him on the neck and whispered, "Good boy—just what he deserves!"

At that exact moment the floor shuddered gently beneath my feet, the windows rattled piteously, and I heard a distant and powerful rumble. Lel lifted his head and pricked his ears up. I glanced automatically at my watch: two minutes after ten. I waited, my whole body tense. The rumble did not repeat itself. Somewhere above me a door slammed heavily, rattling the kitchen pots. Kaisa said, "Oh my god!" loudly. I stood up, but by then I could hear the sound of footsteps, and the owner came in carrying two cups of hot liquor.

"Did you hear that?" he asked.

"Yes. What was it?"

"An avalanche in the mountains. Not too far away either . . . Excuse me for a second, Peter."

He put the glasses down on the mantelpiece and left the

room. I picked up my glass and sat back down in my chair. I felt completely calm. Landslides didn't scare me, and the port, which had been infused with lemon and cinnamon, was beyond praise. Excellent, I thought, settling in.

"Excellent!" I said out loud. "Right, Lel?"

Lel didn't object, even though he hadn't tried any of the hot port.

The owner came back. He picked up his glass, sat down beside me and stared at the embers for some time.

"It doesn't look good, Peter," he said finally, with heavy solemnity. "We're cut off from the outside."

"What do you mean?" I asked.

"How long does your vacation last, Peter?" he continued in the same dull voice.

"Until around the twentieth. Why do you ask?"

"The twentieth," he said slowly. "More than two weeks . . . In that case, it looks like you should be able to get back on time."

I put my glass on my knee and repaid his mystifications with a sarcastic look.

"Out with it, Alek," I said. "Don't pull any punches. What's happened? Has HE finally returned?"

The owner flashed a placating grin.

"No. Not yet, thank god. I have to tell you—just between us—that HE was quite a moody and grumpy type of person, and if HE did ever return . . . However, let's not speak poorly about the dead. Let's talk about the living. I'm glad you have two weeks left, because it may take them that long to dig us out."

Now I understood.

"The road's blocked?"

"Yes. Just now I tried to get in touch with Mur. The telephone isn't working. That can mean only one thing, the same thing that it's meant several times in the past ten years: an avalanche has blocked Bottleneck. You passed that way yourself. It's the only way into my valley."

He took a sip from his glass.

"I realized what had happened immediately," he continued. "The rumble came from the north. Now all we can do is wait. Wait for them to remember us and organize a work crew . . ."

"We've got more than enough water," I said thoughtfully. "But what's to prevent us from descending into cannibalism?"

"There'll be no need for that," the manager said complacently. "Only if you want to spice up the menu. Except I'm warning you up front: I won't give you Kaisa. You can gnaw on Du Barnstoker. He won seventy crowns off me tonight, the old cheat."

"How about fuel?" I asked.

"There's always my perpetual motion machines."

"Hmm . . ." I said. "Are they made of wood?"

The owner gave me a reproachful look. Then he said:

"Why haven't you asked about the booze, Peter?"

"What about the booze?"

"When it comes to booze, we're doing very well," the owner said proudly. "A hundred and twenty bottles—and that's only the house liqueur."

We stared at the embers for a while, sipping quietly at our drinks. I was as happy as I'd ever been. I thought about what might come of this, and the more I thought about it, the more I liked it.

Suddenly the owner spoke.

"The only thing that bothers me, Peter, if we can be serious for a moment, is that I think I've lost a good client."

"What makes you think that?" I asked. "So far as I can see you have eight tasty flies in your web, and now they have no chance of escaping for another two weeks. Now that's what I call good publicity! When it's all over, they'll talk about how they were buried alive and almost had to eat one another . . ."

"That's true," the manager said with satisfaction. "The thought had occurred to me already. But there would be even more flies if Hinkus's friends managed to make it here . . ."

"Hinkus's friends?" I said, surprised. "He told you that he had friends who were coming?"

"Not told me, exactly . . . He called the telegraph office in Mur and dictated a telegram."

"And . . . ?"

The manager raised a finger and recited solemnly.

"'IN MUR, AT THE DEAD MOUNTAINEER'S INN. WAITING. HURRY.' Something like that."

"I would never have guessed," I muttered. "Hinkus has friends who are willing to share his solitude. But then again, why not? *Pourquoi pas*, as they say . . ."

7.

By midnight the owner and I had a pitcher of hot port already under our belts, and had moved on from discussing how best to notify the guests that they had been buried alive to more universal questions—for example, Is mankind doomed to extinction (Yes, doomed, but we won't be around when it happens); Is there a force in nature that the human mind cannot fathom (Yes, there is, but we'll never know anything about it); Is Lel the St. Bernard capable of sentient thought (Yes, he is, though convincing scientific dolts of this is impossible); Is the universe in danger of succumbing to so-called "heat death" (No, it is not in danger, due to the existence of perpetual motion machines of both the first and second type in the owner's barn); Was Brun a boy or a girl (Here I was unable to come to any conclusion, but the owner put forward the odd idea that Brun was a zombie, that is, a sexless creature animated by magic) . . .

Kaisa was cleaning in the dining room; she had washed all the dishes and presented herself to ask if she could go to bed. We let her go. Watching her as she went, the owner complained about his loneliness, and the fact that his wife had left him. That is to say, she hadn't left him . . . it wasn't as simple as that . . . but, in a word, to speak plainly, he was currently wifeless. I told him not to marry Kaisa, first because it would

hurt business, and second because Kaisa loved men too much
to make a good wife. The owner agreed that this was true, he
had thought about it a long time himself and come to the same
conclusions. Still, he said, who am I supposed to marry now
that we're going to be buried in this valley for the rest of our
lives? I was unable to give him any advice on that score; all I
did was admit that I was on my second marriage, and therefore had probably already taken more than my share. It was a
terrible way to think about it, and although the owner forgave
me immediately, I still felt like an egoist and bad Samaritan.
In order to repay him in some way for all my awful attributes,
I decided to school him in the technicalities of forging lottery tickets. He listened attentively, but this didn't seem like
enough to me, so I demanded that he write it down. "You'll
forget!" I repeated despairingly. "You'll sober up and forget
all about it . . ." The owner grew terribly afraid that he really
would forget it, and demanded that we give it a practice run.
I think it was around then that Lel the St. Bernard suddenly
jumped up and gave a deep bark. The owner stared at him.

"I don't understand!" he said sternly.

Lel barked twice and went out into the lobby.

"Aha," said the owner, standing up. "Someone's arrived."

We followed Lel. We were flush with the spirit of hospitality. Lel was standing by the front door. Strange scratching and
whining sounds were coming from the other side. I grabbed
the owner's hand.

"Bear!" I whispered. "A grizzly. Do you have a gun?
Quickly!"

"That's no bear, I'm afraid," the owner said in his dull voice.
"It's HIM. At last. We need to unlock it."

"We do not!" I said.

"We do. He paid for two full weeks, but only stayed one.
We have no right. They'll take away my license."

The sound of scraping and whimpering came from behind the door. Lel was acting strangely: he stood with his side to the door, staring at it with an inquisitive expression, and giving the air a big sniff from time to time. In my opinion, this was exactly how a dog would behave when confronted with a ghost for the first time. While I was searching agonizingly for a good reason not to open the door, the owner came to his own decision. He bravely reached out and slid the bolt open.

The door opened, and a snow-caked figure slowly collapsed at our feet. All three of us rushed towards him, dragging him into the lobby and turning him onto his back. The snow-caked man groaned and stretched out. His eyes were closed and his long nose was white.

Without losing a second, the owner burst into a frenzy of activity. He woke up Kaisa, ordered her to heat up some water, poured a glass of hot port down the stranger's throat, rubbed his face with a wool mitten, and then announced that we needed to get him in the shower. "Peter—armpits," he ordered. "I'll get the legs." I carried out his order, experiencing no small shock when I saw that the stranger was missing an arm, his right one, up to the shoulder. We dragged the poor guy into the shower and lay him on the bench, at which point Kaisa ran in wearing only a nightgown, and the owner told me that he would take it from here.

I went back to the fireplace and finished my port. My head was totally clear; I was capable of analyzing and comparing events with unusual speed. The stranger's clothes were out of season. A short jacket, flared pants and dress shoes. Only someone who was traveling by car would wear something like that to a place like this. Which means that something had happened to the car, and he'd been forced to make his way to the inn on foot. No doubt over quite a distance, considering how exhausted and cold he looked. Then I understood. It

was obvious: he'd been coming here by car, and got hit by the
avalanche at Bottleneck. So this was Hinkus's friend! We had
to wake up Hinkus . . . Maybe there were still people back at
the car, who'd been wounded and couldn't move. Maybe they
were already dead . . . Hinkus had to know . . .

I ran out of the den and up to the second floor. As I passed
the shower, I heard the water gushing fiercely and the owner
chastising Kaisa for her stupidity in a fierce whisper. The hallway light was out; I spent quite a while finding the switch, and
then even longer knocking on Hinkus's door. Hinkus wasn't
answering. Well, then, he must still be on the roof! I was hor-
rified. Had he fallen asleep up there? What if he'd frozen! I
rushed frantically up the attic stairs . . . there he was, sitting on
the roof. He was sitting in the same position as before, bundled up, with his head hidden in the huge collar and his hands
pulled into their sleeves.

"Hinkus!" I shouted.

He didn't move. I ran up to him and shook his shoulder.
I couldn't believe it. Hinkus collapsed, gently giving way beneath my hand.

"Hinkus!" I cried in agitation, involuntarily trying to
catch him.

The coat opened, and out fell some clumps of snow and
the fur hat; only then did I realize that this wasn't Hinkus: it
was just a snowman with his fur coat wrapped around it. That
was the moment when I sobered up at last. I looked quickly
around me. The small bright moon was hanging directly over
my head, and I could see everything, as if it were day. There
were many sets of footprints on the roof, but they were all the
same: it was impossible to tell whose was whose. The snow
beside the chaise longue had been trampled, scattered and
dug through—maybe because of a scuffle, maybe in order to
gather snow for the snowman. The snow-covered valley was

white and clear as far as the eye could see, the dark stripe of the road led north before disappearing in the blue-gray fog that was hiding the mouth of Bottleneck.

Stop, I thought, attempting to get a hold of myself. Let's try and figure out why Hinkus needed all these props. He wanted to make us think he was sitting on the roof, of course. Meanwhile, he'd been somewhere else, doing something completely different . . . the tuberculosis was fake, he wasn't such a sad-sack . . . But what was he doing, and where? I examined the roof again thoroughly, attempting to make some sense of the footprints, but I couldn't understand anything; I searched through the snow but found only a pair of bottles— one of which was empty, and the other of which still had a little brandy in it. It was the undrunk brandy that really got to me. I knew that things had to be really serious if Hinkus was willing to throw away five crowns' worth of brandy. I slowly went back down to the second floor; I knocked on Hinkus's door again, and again no one answered. Just in case, I tried the handle. The door opened. Ready for anything, and with my hand held out in front of me in order to ward off any possible attacks from the darkness, I went in and, after fumbling hurriedly for the switch, turned on the light. Everything in the room looked the same as it had been before: the trunks stood in their old places, though both of them were open. Hinkus wasn't there, of course: but I hadn't expected to find him here. I sat down next to the trunks and carefully went through them again. They were also exactly as they had been, with one small exception: the gold watch and Browning were both gone. If Hinkus had fled, he would have taken the money. It was a good-sized wad, heavy. That meant he was here. Or, if he'd left, that he intended to return.

One thing was clear to me: a crime was about to be committed. What kind of crime? A murder? Burglary? I quickly rejected the idea of murder. I simply couldn't imagine anyone killing anybody here, or think of why they'd do it. But then I remembered the note that they'd slipped Du Barnstoker, and began to feel sick. Though it was clear from the note that they would only kill Du Barnstoker if he tried to run away . . .

I turned off the light and went out into the hallway, closing the door behind me. I went to Du Barnstoker's room and tried the handle. The door was locked. Then I knocked. No one answered. I knocked a second time and put my ear against the keyhole. Vaguely, an obviously half-asleep Du Barnstoker's voice called back: "One minute, I'm just . . ." The old man was not only alive, he wasn't preparing his escape. I didn't want to have to explain myself to him, so I jumped into the stairwell and pressed myself against the wall beneath the attic stairs. A minute later I heard the key snap, and the door creak. Du Barnstoker's voice said, in amazement, "Strange . . ." The door creaked again, the key clicked. Everything was okay—at least for now.

No, I decided finally. Murder was impossible, of course, and the note had been planted either as a joke or as a red herring. But what about robbery? Who was worth robbing here? So far as I could tell, there were two wealthy people in the inn: Moses and the owner. Okay. All right. Both lived on the first floor. The Moseses' room was in the southern wing, the owner's safe was in the northern one. They were divided by a lobby. If I set myself up in the lobby . . . Then again, you could get to the owner's office from upstairs, by coming down from the dining room into the kitchen, and then the pantry. If I secured the pantry door . . . It's settled then: I'll spend the night in the lobby, and tomorrow we'll see. Suddenly I remembered the one-armed stranger. Hmm . . . Now that I think about it, being a friend of Hinkus's, he's probably in on it. Maybe he got in a real accident, but maybe this is all a farce, like the snowman on the roof . . . No, you won't fool us, sir!

I went down the hall. Nobody was in the shower, but Kaisa was standing in the middle of the lobby with an addled look on her face, wearing her nightgown (the skirt of which was wet) and holding the stranger's wet and crumpled clothes in her arms. In the corridor of the southern wing a light was on; from an empty room opposite the den I could hear the muffled bass voice of the owner. He had apparently set the stranger up in here, which was probably just what the one-armed man wanted. It had been smartly done: nobody would drag a half-dead man up to the second floor . . .

Kaisa came to herself finally and started making her way off to the owner's quarters, but I stopped her. I took the clothes from her and searched through the pockets. To my great surprise, there was nothing in the pockets. Absolutely nothing. No money, no identifying documents, no cigarettes, no handkerchief—nothing.

"What's he wearing now?" I asked.

"How do you mean?" Kaisa asked. I didn't press it.

I gave the clothes back and went to see for myself. The stranger was in bed, wrapped in blankets up to his chin. The manager was feeding him something hot with a spoon, saying, "You have to work up a sweat, sir, you have to, you have to get a good sweat going . . ." In all fairness, the stranger looked terrible. His face was blue, the end of his pointy nose was white as snow; one eye was squinting painfully, the other was shut completely. With every breath he let out a feeble moan. If he's someone's accomplice, he's not doing a very good job of it. Still, I had a few questions to ask him. Just in case.

"Did you come here alone?" I asked.

He looked at me with his squinting eye, and moaned quietly:

"Is anyone still in the car?" I asked, enunciating my words. "Or were you traveling alone?"

The stranger opened his mouth, took a small breath and then closed his mouth again.

"He's weak," said the owner. "His body's like a bundle of rags."

"Dammit," I muttered. "And now someone has to go to Bottleneck."

"Yes," agreed the owner. "What if someone was left behind . . . They might have gotten trapped under the avalanche."

"You'll have to go," I said decisively, and at that moment the stranger spoke.

"Olaf," he said expressionlessly. "Olaf And-va-ra-fors . . . Get him."

I felt another shock.

"Aha," said the owner and set the mug of liquid on the table. "I'll get him right away."

"Olaf . . ." the stranger repeated.

When the owner left, I took his place. I felt like an idiot. At the same time, I was pretty relieved: the depressing plot that I'd worked to a point of believability had collapsed.

"Were you alone?" I asked again. "Was anyone else hurt?"

"One . . ." the stranger groaned. "An accident . . . call Olaf . . . where is Olaf Andvarafors?"

"He's here, he's here," I said. "He's coming soon."

He closed his eyes and grew quiet. I leaned back in the chair. Well, all right. But then what had become of Hinkus? And how is the owner's safe doing? My brain had turned to mush.

The owner returned with his eyebrows raised and his lips pursed. He leaned towards my ear and whispered:

"Peter, it's the strangest thing. Olaf isn't answering. His door is locked, there's a draft coming from underneath it.

And my spare keys seem to have gone missing somewhere . . ."

I quietly took from my pocket the bunch that I'd stolen from his office, and handed them to him.

"Ah," the owner said. He took the keys. "Well, anyway. You know, Peter, maybe we should go together. Something doesn't seem right to me . . ."

"Olaf," the stranger groaned. "Where's Olaf?"

"Soon, soon," I told him. My cheek had started to twitch. The owner and I went out into the corridor. "Here, Alek," I said. "Call Kaisa. Have her sit next to this guy and not move until we come back."

"Ah," the owner said again, wiggling his eyebrows. "So that's how it is . . . Something's afoot . . ."

He jogged down to his quarters, and I slowly made my way to the stairs. I'd already gone a few steps when the owner said sternly behind me:

"Come on, Lel. Sit here . . . Sit. Don't let anyone by. No one."

I was already in the second floor hallway by the time he caught up with me, and together we went to Olaf's room. I knocked, seeing just as I did so a note pinned to the door. The note was stuck with a pin right at eye level. "I WAS THERE, AS WE ARRANGED, BUT YOU WERE NOT. IF YOU STILL DESIRE REVENGE, I AM AT YOUR DISPOSAL UNTIL ELEVEN O'CLOCK. DU B."

"Did you see that?" I asked the owner quickly.

"Yes. I just didn't get a chance to tell you."

I knocked again and, not waiting for a reply, grabbed the bunch of keys from the owner.

"Which one is it?" I asked.

The owner pointed it out. I stuck the key in the keyhole. Just my luck: the door was locked from the inside, and some-one had left the key in it. While I worked at it, pushing, the door to the next room over opened and a sleepy and calm-looking Du Barnstoker came out into the hall, tightening the belt of his bathrobe.

"What's going on, gentlemen?" he asked, "Is it now prohibited for the guests to get some sleep?"

"A thousand apologies, Mr. Du Barnstoker," the owner said. "But events have occurred that require decisive action."

"Is that so?" Du Barnstoker said with interest. "I hope I'm not interrupting."

I managed to make a clear path for the key, and straightened up. From beneath the door a winter chill emerged, and I was totally sure that the room would be empty, just like Hinkus's. I turned the key and opened the door. A wave of cold air washed over me, but I hardly felt it. The room was not empty. A man was lying on the floor. The light from the hallway wasn't enough to see who it was. All I saw were the soles of two gigantic shoes on the entryway threshold. I stepped into the entryway and turned on the light.

It was Olaf Andvarafors, manly god and descendent of ancient Scandinavian kings. He was clearly, utterly dead.

8.

After making sure to lock each of the window latches, I picked up his suitcase and, stepping carefully over the body, went out into the hallway. The owner was already waiting for me with glue and strips of paper. Du Barnstoker hadn't left, he was still standing there with his shoulder propped against the wall. He looked twenty years older. His aristocratic jowls drooped and quivered pitifully.

"Horrible!" he muttered, staring at me with despair. "A nightmare . . . !"

I locked the door and sealed it with the five strips of paper, each of which I signed twice.

"Horrible! . . ." Du Barnstoker muttered behind me. "Now there won't be a rematch . . . nothing . . ."

"Go back to your room," I told him. "Lock yourself in and stay there until I call you . . . Wait a second. Was the note yours?"

"It was mine," Du Barnstoker said. "I . . ."

"All right, we'll deal with that later," I said. "Go on." I turned to the owner. "I need to take both your sets of keys. There aren't any more, are there? Good. I need you to do something for me, Alek. Don't tell our one-armed visitor about this. Make something up if he gets too restless. Look in the garage, see if all the cars are where they should be . . . And one more thing:

if you see Hinkus, don't let him leave—even if you have to use force. That's it for now. I'll be in my room. And not a word to anyone, understand?"

The owner nodded his head without saying anything and went downstairs.

Back in my room I set Olaf's suitcase on the filthy table and opened it. Here, too, nothing seemed right. It was even worse than Hinkus's dummy suitcase. At least that had had rags and books in it. But there was only one thing inside this flat and elegant suitcase, and that was some sort of device: a black metal box with a rough surface, some multi-colored buttons, little glass panels with nickel-plated verniers on them . . . No underwear, no pajamas, no soap dish . . . I closed the suitcase, collapsed back into the armchair and lit a cigarette.

All right. What do we have here, Inspector Glebsky? Instead of deep sleep between clean sheets. Instead of getting up early so you can take a snow bath and ski around the whole valley. Instead of eating a good dinner and then indulging in a game of pool, and flirting with Mrs. Moses, and in the evening installing yourself comfortably by the fireplace with a glass of hot port. Instead of enjoying every day of your first real vacation in four years . . . What do we have instead of all this? We have a fresh corpse. Cold-blooded murder. Crime's tedious confusion.

All right. At twenty-four minutes past midnight on the third of March of this year, I, Police Inspector Glebsky, in the presence of the good citizens Alek Snevar and Du Barnstoker discovered the dead body of one Olaf Andvarafors. The corpse was found in the room of the aforementioned Andvarafors; the room was locked from the inside, but the window was wide open. The body was lying facedown, stretched out on the floor. The head of the dead man was turned one hundred and eighty degrees in a brutal and unnatural fashion, so that, even though the body was lying facedown, its face was turned towards the ceiling. The hands of the dead man were extended towards, and had almost reached, the small suitcase that was the only piece of luggage belonging to the deceased. The victim's right hand was clutching a necklace made out of wooden beads, which belonged, as is well known, to the good citizen Kaisa. The features of the victim were distorted, his eyes were wide, his mouth was open. An acrid chemical smell, either from carbolic or formalin, was noted around the mouth. No specific and unambiguous signs of a struggle were present in the room. The bed linen was rumpled, the closet door was open, the heavy chair meant in these rooms to stay at the table had been moved. Traces on the windowsill, or for that matter the snow-covered ledge, could not be found. No traces on the key itself (I took the key out of my pocket and examined it closely again) . . .Visual inspection of the key did not reveal any marks. Due to the lack of technicians, instruments and a lab, medical and fingerprint examination, as well as all other forms of specialized investigation are not possible (and will not be possible). Taking everything into account, death resulted from Olaf Andvarafors's neck being twisted with enormous force and brutality.

I had no idea what to make of the strange odor coming from his mouth, not to mention how much strength the killer must have possessed in order to twist this giant's neck without causing a long and noisy struggle that left behind many traces. But then as everyone knows, multiply two negatives together and you get a positive. It was possible to assume that Olaf had been first given poison, putting him in some sort of helpless state, at which point he was finished off in this brutal manner—a feat that would have required quite a bit of strength on its own, by the way. Yes, this hypothesis explained one thing, though in doing so it immediately raised new questions. Why finish off an incapacitated victim in such a violent and difficult way? Why not just stab him with a knife or wrap a rope around his neck, if worst came to worst? Rage, bloodlust, hatred, revenge? . . . Sadism? . . . Hinkus? All right, maybe it was Hinkus, although Hinkus looked too rubbery for that kind of exertion . . . Or maybe it wasn't Hinkus, but whoever had written me the note about Hinkus? . . .

It didn't make any sense. Why couldn't this be about a fake lottery ticket or doctored account book? Those I could have sorted out quickly . . . This is what I had to do: I had to get in the car and drive until I reached Bottleneck; from there I would try to make my way on skis. I'd reach Mur and come back with the boys from homicide. I even stood up, but then I sat down again. It was a good way out, of course, but it would have had bad consequences. To leave everyone here to their own devices, giving the killer time and possibilities . . . to leave Du Barnstoker, who'd been threatened . . . And anyway, how was I supposed to make it work? You can imagine for yourself what an avalanche in Bottleneck would look like.

There was a knock on the door. The owner came in, carrying a tray with hot coffee and sandwiches on it.

"All the cars are here," he said, setting the tray down in front of me. "The skis too. There's no sign of Hinkus anywhere. His coat and hat are up on the roof—but you've probably seen those already."

"I have," I said, as I sipped the coffee. "And what about the one-armed man?"

"He's sleeping," the owner said. He put his lips together and pressed his fingers against the seams of spilled glue on the table. "Yes . . . He's asleep all right. A strange guy. His color has come back, and he already looks pretty good. I put Lel in with him, just in case."

"Thank you, Alek," I said. "You can go now, and let's keep everything quiet. Let everyone sleep."

The owner shook his head.

"That's not going to work. Moses is already up, his light's on . . . Well, I'll be going, at least I can lock up Kaisa, she's an idiot. Although she doesn't know anything so far."

"Keep it that way," I said.

The owner left. I savored my coffee, pushing the sandwich plate away as I lit another cigarette. When was the last time I saw Olaf? I was playing pool, he was dancing with the kid. That was before the card game had broken up. And then they left, when the clock struck half past . . . something. Immediately after that Moses announced that it was time for him to go to bed. Well, it wouldn't be hard to figure out when that was. But then, how long before that had I seen Olaf for the last time? Maybe not that long. All right, we'll work on that. Now, what about Kaisa's necklace, Du Barnstoker's note, whether or not Olaf's neighbors—Du Barnstoker and Simone—had heard anything . . .

I had just started feeling that I was putting some sort of a picture together, when suddenly I heard a dull, quite heavy thud against the wall bordering the memorial room. I groaned slightly in anger. I threw my jacket off, rolled up my sleeves and tiptoed carefully out into the corridor. One for the kisser, then a slap on each cheek, I thought briefly. I'll give him a practical joke, whoever it was . . .

I opened the door and flew like a bullet into the memorial room. It was dark and I quickly flipped the light switch. The noise stopped suddenly; the room was empty, but I had the feeling that someone was in here. I examined the bathroom, the closet, the curtains. There was a dull moan behind me. I jumped towards the table and hurled a heavy armchair out of the way.

"Get out of there!" I ordered fiercely.

Another dull groan answered me. I squatted, peering under the table. There, wedged between the table-legs in a terribly uncomfortable-looking position—bound with a rope, doubled over and with a gag in his mouth—was the terrifying gangster, maniac and sadist Hinkus, staring at me with dark, tear-filled, suffering eyes. I dragged him into the middle of the room and removed the gag from his mouth.

"What happened?" I asked.

He answered me with a cough. He coughed for a long time, painfully; he was spitting all over the place, groaning and hacking. I looked in the bathroom, got the Dead Mountaineer's razor and cut his ropes. The poor guy was so numb that he couldn't even raise his hands to wipe his face off. I gave him some water. He drank it greedily, until finally he got his voice back and uttered a complicated curse. I helped him stand up and led him over to the armchair. Muttering profanity, his face distorted pitifully, he began rubbing his neck, his wrists, his hips.

"What happened to you?" I asked. Looking at him, I felt relieved: for whatever reason, the idea of Hinkus as a secret murderer had really disturbed me.

"What happened . . . ?" he muttered. "See for yourself! Tied up like a sheep, shoved under a table . . ."

"Who did this?"

"How should I know?" he said angrily, shaking suddenly all over. "Christ!" he muttered. "I need a drink . . . You don't have anything to drink, Inspector?"

"No," I said. "But I'll get something. Just as soon as you answer my questions."

He lifted his left hand up with difficulty and pulled back the sleeve.

"Dammit, the bastard crushed my watch," he muttered. "What time is it, Inspector?"

"One in the morning," I answered.

"One in the morning," he repeated. "One in the morning…" His eyes stared. "No," he said, and stood up. "I need a drink. I'm going down to the pantry to have a drink."

I sat him back down with a light push on his chest.

"There's plenty of time for that," I said.

"I'm telling you, I want a drink!" he said, raising his voice as he tried to stand up again.

"And I'm telling you, that there's plenty of time for that!" I said, pushing him back again.

"What gives you the right to order me around?" He screamed at the top of his voice.

"Don't shout," I said. "I'm a police inspector. And you, Hinkus, are a suspect."

"A suspect of what?" he asked, lowering his voice.

"You know what," I said. I was trying to buy some time, in order to figure out what my next move was.

"I don't know anything," he said gloomily. "Why are you fooling around with me? I don't know anything, and I don't want to know anything. And you'll be sorry for horsing around like this."

I also felt that I would be sorry for horsing around like this.

"Listen, Hinkus," I said. "There's been a murder in the inn. So I suggest you answer my questions, because if you cross me, I'll squash you like a bug. I've got nothing to lose here— in for a penny, in for a pound."

He stared at me quietly for a while, his mouth open.

"A murder…" he repeated, as if disappointed. "Here! And you think I have something to do with it? Me, who was very nearly killed… Who was murdered?"

"Who do you think?"

"How should I know? When I left the dining room, every-one was still alive. And after that…" he was quiet.

"Well?" I asked. "And after that?"

"And after that nothing. I was sitting by myself on the roof, taking a nap. Suddenly I was being grabbed by the neck, someone threw me down, and after that I don't remember anything. I woke up under this lousy table, going crazy almost—I thought I'd been buried alive. I started knocking. I knocked and knocked, but no one came. Then you came. That's it."

"Are you able to say roughly when you were abducted?"

He thought about it for a few minutes, sitting in silence. Then he wiped his mouth with his hand, looked at his fingers, shuddered again, and wiped his hand on his pant leg.

"Well?" I asked.

He looked at me with dull eyes.

"What?"

"I asked, roughly when . . ."

"Right, right: sometime around nine. The last time I looked at my watch it was eight forty."

"Give me your watch," I said.

He obediently unbuckled the watch and held it out to me. I noticed that his wrist was covered with purple-blue spots.

"It's broken," he explained.

The watch wasn't broken: it was crushed. The hour hand was broken off, but the minute hand showed forty-three minutes past the hour.

"Who was it?" I asked again.

"How should I know? I told you I was napping."

"And you didn't wake up when they grabbed you?"

"They were behind me," he said gloomily. "I don't have eyes in the back of my head."

"Wait—look at me!"

He glanced at me sullenly out of the corner of his eyes, and I knew I was on the right track. I held his jaw between my finger and thumb and jerked his head up. I had no idea what those bruises and scratches on his lean, sinewy neck meant, but I spoke confidently.

"Stop lying, Hinkus. He was in front of you, and you saw him. Who was it?"

He freed his head with a jerk.

"Go to hell," he croaked. "Straight to hell. It's none of your damned business. Whoever was murdered here, I didn't have anything to do with it, and everyone else can go to hell too . . . And I need a drink!" he roared suddenly. "I hurt all over, do you understand that, you police pig?"

He was right, so far as I could see. Whatever else he was involved in, the murder had nothing to do with him—at least not directly. However, I had no right to give up now.

"If that's what you want," I said coldly. "Then I'm going to have to lock you in the closet, and there'll be no brandy or cigarettes until you tell me everything you know."

"What do you want from me?" he groaned. I could see that he was close to tears. "Why are you hassling me?"

"Who grabbed you?"

"Dammit!" he whispered despairingly. "Can't you understand that I don't want to talk about it? I saw him—okay, I saw who it was!" He winced again, twisting himself away from me. "I wouldn't want my worst enemy to see what I saw! You, damn you, I wouldn't want you to see it! You'd drop dead from fear!"

He was starting to fall apart.

"All right," I said, standing up. "Come on."

"Where are we going?"

"To get something to drink," I said.

We went into the corridor. He was wobbly, he clung to my sleeve. I was interested to see how he would react to the tape around Olaf's door—but he didn't notice anything. Clearly his mind was elsewhere. I took him into the pool room, found the brandy on the windowsill, which still had half a bottle left from last night, and gave it to him. He grabbed the bottle greedily and took a long swig from it.

"Goddammit," he croaked, wiping his mouth off. "Now that's more like it!"

I watched him. It was possible, of course, that he was in cahoots with the killer, that he'd thought all this up as a diversion (especially since he'd come here with Olaf)—even, that he himself was the murderer and that his accomplices had tied him up afterwards in order to give him an alibi. This seemed too complicated to be true; at the same time, there was no denying that something didn't seem right about him: he clearly didn't have tuberculosis, he didn't act anything like a youth counselor, and there was still the question of what he'd been doing up on the roof . . . Then it hit me! Whatever he'd been doing on the roof, someone hadn't liked it—maybe because it had interfered with Olaf's murder. So they'd gotten rid of him. They'd gotten rid of him, and whoever had done it had somehow given Hinkus a terrible scare, which meant that they weren't guests at the inn, since Hinkus was clearly not afraid of anyone at the inn. It was some kind of mess . . . And then I remembered the part about the shower, and the pipe, and the mysterious notes . . . and I thought about how green and terrified Hinkus had looked that afternoon, coming down from the roof . . .

"Listen, Hinkus," I said softly. "The person who grabbed you . . . You saw him earlier this afternoon, didn't you?"

He glanced at me wildly and took another swig from the bottle.

"All right, then," I said. "Let's go. I'm locking you in your room. You can take the bottle with you."

"What about you?" he said hoarsely.

"What about me?"

"Are you going to leave?"

"Of course."

"Listen," he said. "Listen, Inspector . . ." His eyes were restless, he was searching for the right words. "You . . . I . . . You . . . Check in on me, okay? Maybe I'll remember something else . . . Or maybe I can stay with you?" He stared at me pleadingly. "I won't try to escape, I . . . nothing . . . I swear . . ."

"You're afraid of being left alone in your room?" I asked.

"Yes," he said.

"But I'm going to lock you in," I said. "And I'll keep the key with me . . ."

He waved his hands in desperation.

"That won't help," he said.

"Come on, Hinkus," I said sternly. "Buck up! You're acting like a scared old biddy."

He didn't say anything but only hugged the bottle tenderly against his chest with both hands. I took him to his room and, after promising one more time that I'd check in on him, locked the door. I really did take the key and put it in my pocket. I felt that whatever was going on with Hinkus, it wasn't over yet, and that I'd be dealing with him again. I didn't leave right away. I stood for a few minutes in front of the door, with my ear against the keyhole. I could hear liquid being poured, then the creaking of the bed, then a repetitive noise. I couldn't make out what it was at first, but then I understood: Hinkus was crying.

I left him alone with his conscience and made my way to Du Barnstoker's room. The old man opened his door immediately. He was pretty worked up. He didn't even offer me a seat. The room was full of cigar smoke.

"My dear inspector!" he said quickly, executing a series of elaborate gestures with the cigar that he was holding in two fingers of his outstretched hand. "My esteemed friend!

This is damnably awkward for me to say, but things have gone far enough. I must confess: I have committed a small indiscretion . . ."

"So you killed Olaf Andvarafors," I said glumly, collapsing into the armchair.

He shuddered and threw his hands into the air.

"Good lord! No! I have never raised a finger against anyone in my entire life! *Quelle idée!* No! I only want to confess, with the utmost sincerity, that I have been performing regular mystifications on our inn's guests . . ." He clasped his hands to his chest, sprinkling cigar ashes all over his bathrobe. "Please understand: they were only jokes! Lord knows, not well-executed or intelligent ones, but completely innocent . . . It is my métier, after all, I adore an atmosphere of mystery, mystification, general bewilderment . . . But there was never any *mal* intent, I assure you! I had nothing to gain . . ."

"Exactly what jokes are you talking about?" I asked dryly. I was angry and disappointed. I had not thought that Du Barnstoker would be caught up in all this. I'd expected better of the old man.

"Well . . . All those little jokes about the ghost of the Dead Mountaineer. The, er, shoes that I 'stole' from myself and put under his bed . . . The prank in the shower . . . You were a little taken in by one—remember his pipe ashes? . . . Anyway, things like that, I can't remember them all . . ."

"You ruined my table too?" I asked.

"Table?" he looked at me helplessly, then looked over at his own table.

"Yes, my table. It was covered with glue, a good piece of furniture hopelessly ruined . . ."

"No!" he said fearfully. "Glue . . . a table . . . No, no, that wasn't me, I swear!" He clasped his hands to his chest again. "You must understand, Inspector, I had the best intentions,

not the slightest damage was inflicted . . . I even felt that people were enjoying it—why, our dear inn owner played along
so well . . ."

"The owner was in on it with you?"

"No—how could you think that!" He flapped his hands at
me. "I only mean that he . . . that he, well, he seemed pleased . . .
haven't you noticed that he's a bit of a mystifier himself? You
know, the way he makes his voice sound like that, and then
there's all that 'Allow me to dive into the past . . .'"

"I see," I said. "And the footprints in the corridors?"

Du Barnstoker's face grew focused and serious.

"No, no," he said. "That wasn't me. But I know what you're
talking about. I saw it once. This was before you arrived. Wet
footprints, from bare feet, leading from the landing to—silly
as it sounds—the memorial room . . . Another joke, of course,
though not one of mine . . ."

"All right," I said. "Forget the footprints. I have one more
question. The note that you allegedly received—am I to understand that this was also your work?"

"That wasn't mine either," Du Barnstoker said with dignity.
"When I gave you the note, I was telling the absolute truth."

"Wait a minute," I said. "What you're saying is, Olaf went
out, leaving you sitting by yourself. Then someone knocked
on the door, you went to answer it, and saw that there was a
note on the floor in front of the door. Is that what happened?"

"That's what happened."

"Wait a minute," I said again. I felt a thought coming on.
"Please, Mr. Du Barnstoker, tell me: what made you think that
this threatening letter was addressed to you?"

"I understand what you mean completely," Du Barnstoker
said. "It was only afterwards that I realized—only after reading it did I think that probably, if the note had been meant
for me, it would have been slipped under my door. But at that

moment I acted subconsciously . . . That is to say, whoever knocked must have heard my voice, must have known that I was there . . . Do you see what I'm saying? In any event, when poor Olaf returned, I immediately showed him the note, so that we could both have a good laugh over it . . ."

"All right," I said. "And what about Olaf? Did he laugh?"

"N-no, he didn't . . . His sense of humor, you see . . . He read it, shrugged, and we got right back to the game. He remained perfectly calm and serene and didn't mention the note again . . . As for me, as I told you, I'd decided that someone was playing a joke on us—to be totally honest, I still think that . . . You know that in a narrow circle of bored vacationers, you'll always find one person . . ."

"I know," I said.

"You think the note is authentic?"

"Anything's possible," I said. We were quiet. "Now tell me what you were doing from the moment that the Moseses went to bed."

"Of course," said Du Barnstoker. "I was expecting that question and have gone over the whole series of events in my memory. It happened like this: when everyone had dispersed—it was around nine thirty—I spent some time . . ."

"Just a minute," I interrupted. "You said it was nine thirty?"

"Yes, around that time."

"Good. Then tell me something first. Can you remember who was in the dining room between eight thirty and nine thirty?"

Du Barnstoker took his forehead in his long white fingers.

"Mmm . . ." he said. "That is going to be harder. I was busy with the game . . . Well, naturally, there was Moses, the owner . . . From time to time Mrs. Moses was there picking up the cards for him . . . We were at the table . . . Brun and Olaf danced, and then afterwards . . . No, excuse me, before that

Mrs. Moses and Brun . . . But you must understand, my dear inspector, I cannot possibly be certain when that was—eight thirty, nine . . . Oh! The clock struck nine, and I—I remember—I looked around the hall and thought how few of us were left. The music was playing, but the room was empty. Only Olaf and Brun were dancing . . . You know, unfortunately, this seems to be the only clear impression that has remained in my memory," he concluded with regret.

"So," I said. "Neither the owner nor Moses left the table even once?"

"No," he said confidently. "Both of them turned out to be remarkably zealous gamblers."

"Meaning that at nine o'clock there were only the three gamblers, Brun and Olaf?"

"Precisely. I remember that quite clearly."

"Good," I said. "Now, back to you. After everyone had dispersed, you sat for some time at the card table practicing card tricks . . ."

"Practicing card tricks . . . ? I suppose it's possible . . . Sometimes when I'm lost in thought, you know how it is, my hands take on a will of their own, it happens subconsciously. Indeed. Then I decided to smoke a cigar and made my way back here, to my room. I smoked the cigar, sat in this armchair and dozed off, I have to confess. I was woken up by what felt like a sort of shove—suddenly I remembered that I had promised poor Olaf that I'd give him a chance to get his revenge at ten o'clock. I looked at my watch. I don't remember exactly what the time was, but it was a little after ten, and I felt relieved that I wouldn't be too late. I hastily cleaned myself up in front of the mirror, grabbed a bundle of bills and my cigars and went out into the corridor. It was empty, Inspector—that I remember. I knocked on Olaf's door: nobody answered. I knocked a second time, again without any success. I decided that Mr. Olaf had forgotten about his revenge and found something more interesting to pursue. However, I am terribly scrupulous when it comes to this sort of thing. I wrote the aforementioned note and stuck it to his door. Then I waited until eleven, upon my honor, reading this book here, and at eleven went to bed. And the interesting part of it, Inspector, is that not long before you and the owner started making your racket and clambering up and down the hallway, I was woken up by a knock on my door. I opened it, but no one was there. I went back to bed, but couldn't get to sleep."

"Uh-huh," I said. "I see. What you're saying is that from the moment that you pinned the note until you went to bed at eleven o'clock, nothing else of significance happened . . . there were no noises of any kind, or movement?"

"No," Du Barnstoker said. "Nothing."

"And where were you? Here, or in the bedroom?"

"Here, sitting in this chair."

"Uh-huh," I said. "One last question. Did you talk with Hinkus before lunchtime yesterday?"

"With Hinkus? . . . That ill little . . . Wait a second, my dear friend . . . Of course! We were standing outside the shower, remember? Mr. Hinkus was irritated because we had to wait, and I was calming him with some trick or another . . . Ah yes, the lollipops! He was quite amusingly confused after that. I adore illusions like that."

"And after that you two didn't speak to one another?"

Du Barnstoker pressed his lips together thoughtfully.

"No," he said. "So far as I can remember, not at all."

"And you didn't go up on the roof?"

"On the roof? No. No, no. I didn't go up on the roof."

I stood up.

"Thank you, Mr. Du Barnstoker. I believe this will help the

investigation. I hope you understand how inappropriate further practical jokes would be at this point," (he quietly waved
his hands at me). "Well, that's good. I strongly advise you to
take a sleeping pill and go to bed. In my opinion, that's the best
thing you could do at this point."

"I'll try," Du Barnstoker said.

I wished him a good night and left. I went to wake up the
kid, but then I caught sight of the door to Simone's room shut-
ting quickly and quietly at the end of the hall. I made my way
swiftly back to it.

I went in without knocking and immediately saw that I'd
done the right thing. Through the open bedroom door I saw
the great physicist, hopping on one leg, trying to get his pants
off. This was even more ridiculous given that the lights were
on in both of the rooms.

"Don't bother, Simone," I said grimly. "Anyway, you don't
have time to get your tie off."

Simone collapsed helplessly onto the bed. His jaw was
trembling, his eyes bulged. I went into the bedroom and stood
in front of him, my hands in my pockets. We were quiet for
a while. I didn't say a single word: I only looked at him, giving him time to realize that he was done for. He drooped
even more under my gaze, drawing his head further towards
his shoulders, his knobby, hooked nose looking even more
despondent. Finally he couldn't hold back any longer.

"I will only speak in the presence of my attorney," he announced in a cracking voice.

"Come on, Simone," I said with disgust. "You're a physicist. What kind of lawyer are we going to find for you in this
backwater?"

Suddenly he grabbed my jacket lapel and, looking up into
my eyes, hissed:

"I know what you want, Peter, but I swear, I didn't kill her."

Now it was my turn to take a seat. I groped behind me for a chair and sat down.

"Put yourself in my position—why would I?" Simone continued fervently. "There has to be a motive . . . No one just kills . . . Of course, there are sadists, but they're insane . . . Especially this kind of monstrosity, it's like a nightmare . . . I swear! She was already quite cold when I took her in my arms!"

For a few seconds, I closed my eyes. So there was another dead body in the building. And this time it was a woman.

"You know perfectly well," Simone blabbered on. "Crimes don't just happen. True, André Gide wrote . . . But that's just an intellectual game . . . You need a motive . . . You know me, Peter! Look at me: do I really look like a murderer?"

"Stop," I said. "Shut up for a minute. Think hard and then tell me exactly what happened."

He didn't stop to think.

"Of course," he said readily. "But you have to believe me, Peter. Everything that I'm saying is the sincere truth, and nothing but the truth. That's how it happened. Even during that damned ball . . . She'd given me hints before, though I didn't dare . . . But this time you'd pumped me full of brandy, so I decided, why not? It's not a crime, is it? And then it was eleven o'clock, things were calming down, I left and quietly went downstairs. You and the owner were talking nonsense about the cognition of nature, the usual balderdash . . . I quietly walked past the den—I was wearing socks—and crept to her room. The old man's light was off—hers too. As I'd expected, her door wasn't locked, so right away I was encouraged. It was pitch-dark, but I did make out her silhouette: she was sitting on the couch directly across from the door. I called to her softly, but she didn't answer. Then, well, I sat down next to her and, you know how it is, embraced her . . .

Brr-r-r! . . . I didn't even get a chance to kiss her! She was stone dead . . . hard, stiff . . . Like ice! Like petrified wood! And that grin . . . Who knows how I got out of there. I must have broken all the furniture . . . I swear to you, Peter, take the word of an honest man: when I touched her, she was already completely dead, cold and numb . . . You know I'm not a beast . . ."

"Put your pants on," I said in quiet despair. "Clean yourself up and follow me."

"Where are we going?" he asked in a terrified voice.

"To jail!" I shouted. "Solitary confinement! The torture tower, you idiot!"

"Of course," he said. "Right away. I just didn't understand you, Peter."

Back in the lobby we ran into the owner, who gave me a confused look. He was sitting at a coffee table, on which a heavy Winchester automatic lay. I motioned for him to stay where he was and turned down the corridor towards the Moses's room. Lel, who was lying in the doorway that led to the stranger's room, muttered threateningly at us. Simone trotted after me, sighing dejectedly from time to time.

I pushed the door to Mrs. Moses's room open authoritatively, and stood dumbfounded. The pink lamp in the room was switched on, and on the divan directly across from the door, striking the pose of Madame Récamier, lay the charming Mrs. Moses, in silk pajamas, reading a book. She raised her eyebrows in surprise upon seeing me, but then immediately flashed a sweet smile. Simone behind me let out a weird sound—something like "A-Ap!"

"I beg your pardon," I said, my tongue barely moving in my mouth. I closed the door as quickly as I could. Then I turned to Simone and grabbed his tie.

"I swear!" he mouthed. He was on the verge of fainting.

I let him go.

"You were wrong, Simone," I said dryly. "Let's go back to your room."

We started back the way we came; but along the way I changed my mind and led him to my room. I had suddenly realized that my door wasn't locked, and that I had evidence in there. Also, I thought it might not be a bad idea to show that evidence to the great physicist.

After he'd made it through the door Simone ran over to my chair, covered his face with his hands for a moment, and then began hitting himself on the skull with his fists like an excited chimpanzee.

"I'm saved!" he muttered with an idiotic smile. "Hooray! I can live again! No need to lurk and hide! Hooray! . . ."

He put his hands on the edge of the table and stared up at me with his round eyes. He whispered:

"But she really was dead, Peter! I swear to you. She was dead, someone killed her, and not only that . . ."

"Nonsense," I said coldly. "You were drunk as a skunk, that's all."

"No, no," Simone said, shaking his head. "I was drunk, that's true, but there's something not right about it, something strange . . . It feels more like a nightmare, delirium . . . like a dream . . . Maybe I really do have a screw loose, eh Peter?"

"Maybe," I agreed.

"I don't know, I just don't know . . . My eyes were open the whole time, I took my clothes off, put them back on . . . I even wanted to run . . . especially when I heard you walking down the hall, and when you started speaking in that muffled voice . . ."

"Where were you at that time?"

"I was . . . what time do you mean exactly?"

"When you heard our muffled voices."

"In my room. I didn't leave."

"In precisely what part of the room were you?"

"All over the place, really . . . To be honest, while you were questioning Olaf, I sat in the bedroom and tried to listen in . . ." His eyes suddenly began bulging back out of his head. "Wait a minute," he said. "But if she's still alive, then what's all the fuss about? What happened? Is someone sick?"

"Answer my questions," I said. "What did you do after I left the pool room?"

He was silent for a while, looking at me with his round eyes while he chewed his lower lip.

"I get it," he said finally. "That means something did happen. Well, all right, then . . . What did I do after you left? I shot pool by myself for a while and then went back to my room. It was about ten, I had planned to make my attempt at eleven, and I needed to get myself ready, to freshen up, shave, etc. . . . I did this until around ten thirty. Then I waited around, looking at my watch, staring out the window . . . You know the rest . . ."

"You say you went back to your room around ten. Can you be more specific? You had an appointment to keep, you must have been looking at your watch a lot."

Simone whistled softly.

"Ho-ho," he said. "A real investigation. Can you at least tell me what's happened?"

"Olaf's been killed," I said.

"Killed—how is that possible? You were just in his room . . . I heard you talking to him in there myself . . ."

"I wasn't talking with him," I said. "Olaf is dead. So please, try to recall precisely what I'm asking you about. When did you get back to your room?"

Simone wiped his sweat-covered forehead. He looked miserable.

"This is crazy," he muttered. "Madness . . . First that, now this . . ."

I used an old and reliable trick. Looking fixedly at Simone, I said: "Stop trying to wiggle out of it. Answer my questions."

Put abruptly in the position of a suspect, all of Simone's sentiments vanished. He stopped thinking about Mrs. Moses. He stopped thinking about poor Olaf. Now he was only thinking about himself.

"Why do you say that?" he muttered. "What does that mean, 'stop trying to wiggle out of it'?"

"It means I'm waiting for an answer," I said. "When, exactly, did you get back to your room?"

Simone shrugged his shoulders with exaggerated sulkiness.

"All right," he said. "It's funny, of course, absurd even, but . . . as you wish. As you wish. I left the billiard room at ten minutes to ten. Give or take a minute, to be precise. I looked at my watch and understood that I had to go. Ten minutes to ten."

"What did you do, once you'd gotten back to your room?"

"I went into the bedroom, undressed . . ." Suddenly he stopped. "You know, Peter, I think I understand what you're looking for. At that point Olaf was still alive. Then again, for all I know that might not even have been Olaf."

"One thing at a time," I said.

"There's nothing to tell . . . Behind the bedroom wall, I heard furniture moving. I didn't hear any voices. There weren't any voices. But something was moving. I remember, I stuck my tongue out at the wall and thought: that's right, you blond beast, you go to bed and I'll go to my Olga . . . Or something along those lines. It was around five to ten at that point. Give or take three minutes."

"Okay. And after that?"

"After that . . . ? After that I went into the bathroom. I washed myself thoroughly from the waist up and then dried off thoroughly with a towel. I shaved thoroughly with an electric razor . . . I dressed, thoroughly . . ." More and more sarcasm was emerging from his annoyingly puckish voice. However, he felt immediately how inappropriate such a tone was and corrected himself. "In short, the next time I looked at my watch was when I left the bathroom. It was around ten thirty. Give or take two or three minutes."

"You stayed in the bedroom?"

"Yes, I got dressed in the bedroom. But I didn't hear anything else. Or if I did hear anything, I didn't pay attention. Once I'd gotten dressed, I went into the living room and sat down to wait. And I solemnly swear that I never laid eyes on Olaf again after the party."

"You already solemnly swore that Mrs. Moses was dead," I pointed out. ·

"Well, I don't know . . . I don't understand what happened. I promise, Peter . . ."

"I believe you," I said. "Now tell me, when was the last time you spoke with Hinkus?"

"Hm . . . To tell you the truth, I can honestly say I've never spoken to him. Not once. I can't imagine what we'd have to talk about."

"And when was the last time you saw him?"

Simone's eyes narrowed as he tried to remember.

"Outside the shower?" he said with a questioning intonation. "No—what am I thinking? He had dinner with everyone, you brought him down from the roof. After that . . . he disappeared somewhere, who knows where . . . What happened to him?"

"Nothing special," I said casually. "One more question. Who, in your opinion, has been playing all these practical jokes? The shower, the missing shoes . . ."

"I understand," said Simone. "In my opinion, Du

Barnstoker started them, but then everyone joined in. The owner more than anybody."

"You too?"

"Me too. I looked into Mrs. Moses's windows. I love jokes like that . . ." He started to launch into his morbid laugh, but then caught himself and quickly made a serious face.

"Is there anything else?"

"Well, why wouldn't there be? I would call Kaisa from empty rooms and arrange one of my 'wet walks.'"

"Meaning . . . ?"

"Meaning I ran through the hallways with wet feet. Then I was going to indulge in a little haunting, but I never got around to it."

"Lucky for the rest of us," I said dryly. "And Moses's watch—did you do that?"

"What about Moses's watch? The gold one? The one shaped like a turnip?"

I wanted to hit him.

"Yes," I said. "The turnip. Did you steal it?"

"What do you take me for?" Simone said, outraged. "What do I look like to you, some kind of hoodlum?"

"No, not a hood," I said, maintaining my self-control. "You took one as part of a joke. You staged a 'visit from the Thief of Baghdad.'"

"Listen, Peter," Simone said, turning very serious. "I can see that something must have happened with that watch. I didn't touch it. But I did see it. Everyone did, I'm sure. A huge turnip, which I know because one day Moses dropped it into his mug in front of everyone . . ."

"Fine," I said. "Let's put this aside for a moment. Now I have a question for you as a specialist." I laid Olaf's suitcase in front of him and opened the top. "What could this be, in your opinion?"

Simone quickly examined the device; he pulled it carefully out of the suitcase and, whistling through his teeth, began looking it over from all sides. Then he hefted it in his hands and put it just as carefully back in the suitcase.

"This isn't my field," he said. "Judging by how compact it is, and how well made, I'd say it's either military or space-related. I don't know. I can't even guess. Where did you find it? On Olaf?"

"Yes," I said.

"Who'd have thought!" he muttered. "That big oaf . . . Excuse me. What are the damned verniers for? Well, these are obviously connection jacks . . . A very strange aggregator . . ." He looked at me. "If you want, Peter, I could push the keys here and turn these wheels and screws. I'm a risk taker. But remember, this isn't a healthy thing to be."

"That won't be necessary," I said. "Give it to me." I closed the suitcase.

"You're right," Simone said approvingly, and leaned back in his chair. "It requires a specialist. I don't even know who . . . By the way," he said. "Why are you doing all this? Do you love your job that much? Why don't you call in the experts?"

I told him briefly about the avalanche.

"It never rains . . ." he said morosely. "Can I go?"

"Yes," I said. "And stay in your room. The best thing would be to go to sleep."

He left. I took the suitcase and looked for a place where I could hide it. I couldn't find anywhere. Military, or space, I thought. Just what I needed. A political assassination, a spy, sabotage . . . Come on! If they'd killed him for the suitcase, they would have taken the suitcase . . . Where was I supposed to put it? Then I remembered the owner's safe and, sticking the suitcase under my arm (just to be safe), I went downstairs.

The owner had set himself up at the coffee table with his

papers and an old-fashioned adding machine. His Winchester was leaning up against the wall, ready if he needed it.

"What's new?" I asked.

He stood up to greet me.

"Nothing particularly good," he answered with a guilty look on his face. "I had to explain to Moses what happened."

"Why?"

"He rushed after the two of you with murder in his eyes, hissing that no one was going to break in on his wife. I didn't know how to stop him, so I told him what was going on. I decided that would be less noisy."

"That's not good," I said. "But it's my fault. What did he do?"

"Nothing really. Bugged his eyes out at me, took a swig from his mug, didn't say anything for a few minutes, and then began to shout—who had I lodged in his section, and how did I dare . . . I barely managed to get away."

"That's all right," I said. "Here's what we'll do, Alek. Give me the key to your safe, I'll put the suitcase in there, and the key—you'll have to excuse me—I'll keep with me. Second, I need to question Kaisa. Bring her into your office. Third, I could really use some coffee."

"Come with me," said the manager.

9.

I drank a big cup of coffee and went to question Kaisa. The coffee was excellent. But I got almost nothing out of Kaisa. First off, she kept falling asleep in her chair, and when I woke her up, she immediately asked, "What?" Second, it seemed she was completely incapable of talking about Olaf. Each time I said his name, she blushed red, began to giggle, made a complicated movement with her shoulder and covered herself with one hand. I was left with the unshakable impression that Olaf had been naughty here, and that it had happened almost immediately after dinner, when Kaisa had been clearing and washing the dishes. "But he took my beads," she said, twittering and mooning. "He said they were a souvenir. Something to remember me by. What a troublemaker . . ." In the end, I told her to go to bed, and then went out in the lobby to make my way to the owner.

"What do you think about all this, Alek?" I asked.

He pushed his adding machine out of the way with relish and stretched his powerful shoulders until they cracked.

"I think, Peter, that pretty soon I'm going to have to give this inn another name."

"How so?" I said. "And what name are you thinking of?"

"I don't know yet," the manager said. "But it's bothering me a little. In a few days, this valley of mine will be swarming with reporters; I've got to get all my ducks in order before that happens. Naturally, everything depends on what conclusions the official investigation draws, but then the press will have to listen to the proprietor's thoughts on what happened . . ."

"Does the proprietor already have thoughts on what happened?" I said, surprised.

"Well, maybe it's not quite accurate to call them thoughts . . . In any case, I have experienced certain feelings that you yourself, in my opinion, haven't arrived at yet. But you will, Peter. I have no doubt events will present themselves in the same way to you as you dig deeper into the case. You and I are just built differently. I'm a mechanic, self-taught, which means that I tend to have feelings instead of conclusions. And you—you're a police inspector. Feelings for you arise as a result of your conclusions, when the conclusions you draw are unsatisfying. When they discourage you. That's how I see it, Peter . . . So now, ask your questions."

At that point—because I was very tired and very discouraged—I did something I hadn't expected to do. I told him about Hinkus. He listened, nodding his bald head.

"Yes," he said, when I had finished. "You see, even Hinkus . . ."

Having made this mysterious remark he told me, thoroughly and without any undue emphasis, what he'd done after the card game was over. However, he didn't know much—for example, he'd last seen Olaf around the same time I had. At nine thirty he had gone downstairs with the Moseses, fed Lel, put him out for his walk, told Kaisa off for her tardiness . . . at which point I showed up. The idea to sit by the fireplace with some hot port came up. He gave Kaisa her orders and made his way to the dining room to turn off the music and lights.

"Of course, I could have then made my way up to Olaf and wrung his neck, though I'm not totally sure Olaf would have let me do that. But I didn't even try it; I just went downstairs and turned off the light in the lobby. So far as I can remember, everything was as it should be. All the doors on the top floor were closed, it was quiet. I went back to the pantry, poured the port, and at exactly that minute the avalanche occurred. I brought you the port, thinking to myself, 'I should go call Mur.' I already had the feeling that something bad had happened. After I'd called, I joined you again by the fireplace, from which point on we were together the whole time."

I watched him through half-closed eyelids. He was a very strong man, no doubt about it. Strong enough, probably, to twist Olaf's neck, especially if Olaf had been poisoned ahead of time. After all, as the owner of the inn, he really could have poisoned any of us. Not only that, but he could have had a spare key to Olaf's room. A third key—any of this was possible. But one thing he couldn't have done: he couldn't have left the room through the door and then locked it from the inside. He couldn't have jumped out the window without either leaving marks on the windowsill or the ledge or a trace—a very deep and clear trace—beneath the window . . . So far as I could figure it, no one could have done all that. Which meant that there had to be a secret passage leading from Olaf's room to the room currently occupied by the one-armed man . . . though at that point the crime became highly intricate, which means that it would have had to be planned a long time in advance, in detail, and with absolutely no comprehensible goal . . . Well, hell, I had heard him turn off the music, and walk down the stairs and reprimand Lel. A minute later there was the avalanche, and then . . .

"If you'll indulge my curiosity for a moment," the owner said. "Why did you go with Simone to see Mrs. Moses?"

"No reason really," I said. "The great physicist had drunk too much and was imagining god knows what . . ."

"You won't tell me what it was exactly?"

"It's all nonsense!" I said angrily, trying to catch the tail of the curious idea that had floated into my head a few seconds earlier. "You've clogged my brain with your garbage, Alek . . . Well, all right, I'll remember it later . . . But anyway, back to Hinkus. Try to remember who left the dining room between eight thirty and nine."

"I can try, of course," the manager said casually. "But after all, it was you yourself who drew my attention to the fact that Hinkus was insanely frightened by whomever—or should I say *whatever*—had tied him up."

I stared at him.

"What are you getting at?"

"What are *you* getting at?" he asked. "If I were in your place, I'd be thinking about this quite seriously."

"Are you joking?" I said irritably. "I don't have time right now for mysticism, science fiction or any of your other philosophical fancies. What I think is that Hinkus is . . ." I tapped the side of my temple. "It seems inconceivable to me that someone could have been hiding in the inn without us knowing about it."

"All right, all right," the manager said graciously. "We won't argue about it. So: who left the dining room between nine thirty and ten? First of all, Kaisa. She was going in and out. Second, Olaf. He was also going in and out. Third, Du Barnstoker's child . . . But no. The child disappeared later, together with Olaf . . ."

"When was that?" I asked quickly.

"Naturally, that's the part I can't remember, though I do recall that we were playing cards and kept playing for some time after they'd left."

"Very interesting," I said. "But we'll get to that later. Who else was there?"

"Indeed, yes, only Mrs. Moses is left . . . Hmm . . ." He scratched his nails deeply against his cheek. "No," he said decisively. "I don't remember. As the owner I generally keep track of my guests and therefore, as you see, have quite a good memory about certain things. But you know, I had a pretty lucky stretch there. It didn't last long, maybe two or three hands, but as for what happened during that run . . ." The manager's hands shot up. "I do remember that Mrs. Moses danced with the child, and I remember that afterwards she sat down with us and even played. But whether she left or not . . . No, I didn't see. Unfortunately."

"Thanks anyway," I said distractedly. I was already thinking about something else. "So the child left with Olaf, and they didn't come back, right?"

"Right."

"And that was before nine thirty, when you got up from the card game?"

"Precisely."

"Thank you," I said, and stood up. "I'll go now—just one more question. Did you see Hinkus after dinner?"

"After dinner? No."

"Oh right, you were playing cards . . . How about before dinner?"

"Before dinner I saw him a couple of times. I saw him that morning, at breakfast, then in the yard, when everyone was playing and frolicking around . . . Then he sent a telegram to Mur from my office . . . After that . . . right! After that he asked me how to get up on the roof, he said he wanted to get some sun . . . That's about it, I think. No, I saw him once more during the day, in the pantry, when he was occupied with a bottle of brandy. Other than that I didn't see him during the day."

I thought I'd caught my escaping thought.

"Listen, Alek, I completely forgot," I said. "How did Olaf sign himself in?"

"Should I bring you the book," the manager asked. "Or just tell you?"

"Tell me."

"Olaf Andvarafors, civil servant, on vacation for ten days, alone."

No, that wasn't it.

"Thanks, Alek," I said and sat down again. "Now keep doing what you were doing, I'll just sit here and think."

I put my head in my hands and started to think. What did I have? Not a lot, not a damn lot. I knew that Olaf had left the dining room between nine and nine thirty, and had not returned. I'd discovered that Olaf's companion had been none other than the kid. Which meant, so far as I could see, that the kid was the last person who had seen Olaf alive. If I didn't count the killer, of course. And assuming that everyone I'd interrogated was telling the truth. That meant that Olaf had been killed somewhere between nine and soon after midnight. That was quite a gap. On the other hand, Simone had said that at five minutes to ten he could hear some kind of movement in Olaf's room, and at around ten minutes to eleven Du Barnstoker's knock had gone unanswered. But that still doesn't mean anything, Olaf could have left at that point. I pulled at my hair in frustration. Olaf could have been killed somewhere other than his room . . . No, no, it was too early to draw conclusions. There was still Brun's involvement in Olaf's case to deal with, and Mrs. Moses's involvement in Hinkus's case . . . But then what could she tell me? That I went up on the roof, darling, and then I saw Hinkus . . . But why did she go up on the roof? Alone, without her husband, with her décolletage . . . Right. Question: who do I start with? Since Olaf was dead, not Hinkus, and since Mrs. Moses had probably already heard about the murder from her spouse, let's start with the kid. People say some interesting things when they've just woken up. Besides, I thought as I stood up, I might be able to determine what gender it is.

I had to knock long and loud on the door to the kid's room. Then bare feet shuffled to the door and an angry husky voice demanded to know what the hell I wanted.

"Open the door, Brun, it's me, Glebsky," I said.

A short silence followed this. Then a frightened voice asked.

"Are you, crazy? It's three in the morning!"

I raised my voice. "I told you to open up!"

"What's this about?"

I said the first thing I thought of. "Your uncle doesn't feel well."

"Is this a joke? Wait a second, let me get some pants on . . ."

The slapping bare feet retreated. I waited. Then a key turned in the lock, the door opened, and the kid stepped over the threshold.

"Not so fast," I said, grabbing it by the shoulder. "Back in the room, if you please . . ."

The kid was obviously not fully awake yet and for that reason didn't put up much of a fight. It willingly went back into the room and sat on the rumpled bed. I sat in the armchair across from it. The kid looked at me for a few seconds through its huge black glasses. Suddenly its plump pink lips began to tremble.

"Is it bad?" it asked in a whisper. "Don't keep quiet, tell me something!"

It was no small surprise for me to discover that this wild creature apparently loved its uncle and was frightened that something might have happened to him. I took out a cigarette and lit it.

"Your uncle's fine. We've got other things to talk about."

"But you said . . ."

"I didn't say anything, you were dreaming. So tell me quickly, don't hesitate: when did you and Olaf go your separate ways? Come on, quick!"

"Olaf? What do you mean? What do you want from me?"

"When and where was the last time you saw Olaf?"

The kid shook its head.

"I don't understand any of this. Why are you talking about Olaf? What happened to my uncle?"

"Your uncle's sleeping. He's alive and well. When was the last time you saw Olaf?"

"Why do you keep asking me about that?" the kid said, outraged. Gradually, it came to its senses. "And why did you burst in on me in the middle of the night?"

"I'm asking you . . ."

"Screw your questions! Shove off, or I'll call my uncle! Damned cop!"

"You were dancing with Olaf, and then you left? Where did you go? Why?"

"What's it to you? Jealous about your bride?"

"Quit the nonsense, you pathetic little waif!" I barked. "Olaf has been killed! I know that you were the last one to see him alive! When was it? Where? Quick! Well?"

I must have looked scary. The kid drew back and put its hands out, palms forward, as if to protect itself.

"No!" it whispered. "What are you saying? What . . ."

"Answer me," I said quietly. "You left the dining room with him and went . . . where?"

"N-nowhere . . . We just went out into the corridor . . ."

"And then?"

The kid was quiet. I couldn't see its eyes, which was unusual and unsettling.

"And then?" I repeated.

"Call my uncle," the kid said firmly. "I want my uncle here."

"Your uncle won't be able to help you," I said. "Only one thing can help you: the truth. Tell the truth."

The kid didn't say anything. It sat there, huddled up on the bed beneath a large handwritten sign that read "Let's get violent!" and was quiet. Tears began flowing down its cheeks from under the sunglasses.

"Tears won't help either," I said coldly. "Tell the truth. If you lie and try to twist things around," I put my hand in my pocket, "I'll put you in handcuffs and send you to Mur. There you'll be interrogated by complete strangers. We're talking about murder here—do you understand?"

"I understand . . ." the kid whispered, so softly I could barely hear it. "I'll tell you . . ."

"Good choice," I said approvingly. "So, you and Olaf went into the hallway. Then what?"

"We went into the hallway . . ." the kid repeated mechanically. "And then . . . and then . . . I can't really remember, I have a lousy memory . . . He said something, and I . . . He said something and left, and I . . . that . . ."

"This isn't working," I said, shaking my head. "Let's try again."

The kid sniffled, wiped its nose and put its hand under the pillow. It pulled out a handkerchief.

"Well?" I said.

"It's all . . . it's all so embarrassing," the kid whispered. "And horrible. And Olaf is dead."

"A cop's like a doctor," I said portentously, feeling very awkward. "Words like 'embarrassing' aren't in our vocabulary."

"Well, all right," the kid said suddenly, defiantly raising its head. "Here's what happened. At first it was a joke: bride and groom, girl or boy . . . Anyway, that's about how you treated me . . . He probably felt the same way too, who knows what he took me for . . . And then, after we'd left, he started pawing at me. It was disgusting, I had to give him one . . . right in the face . . ."

"And then?" I asked, not looking at it.

"And then, he was offended, he cursed me out and left. Maybe it wasn't fair of me, maybe I shouldn't have hit him, but he was wrong too . . ."

"Where'd he go?"

"How should I know? He went down the hallway . . ." the kid waved its hand. "I don't know where to."

"What about you?"

"Me? What about me? The mood was ruined, gross, boring . . . Only one thing to do: go back to my room, lock myself in and get drunk as hell . . ."

"So you got drunk?" I asked, sniffing carefully and looking furtively around the room. The mess was awful, junk was scattered everywhere, things were piled up who knew how, and there were long strips of paper on the table—signs, so far as I could tell. To be hung on the cop's door . . . I could actually smell the alcohol, and on the floor next to the head of the bed, I noticed a bottle.

"I told you."

I bent down and picked up the bottle. It was almost empty.

"Someone needs to give you a good spanking, young man," I said, putting the bottle on the table, right on top of the placard bearing the slogan "Down with generalizations! Meet the moment!" "So you were sitting here the whole time?"

"Yes. What's a . . . person supposed to do in that situation?" The kid was apparently still trying, as if by force of habit, to avoid giving itself away.

"When did you go to bed?"

"I don't remember."

"Okay, then, so be it," I said. "Now, can you give me a detailed description of everything you did from the moment you left the table to the moment you and Olaf went out into the hallway."

"Detailed?" the kid asked.

"Yes. As detailed as possible."

"Okay," the kid agreed, showing its small sharp teeth, which were so white they looked blue. "There I am finishing dessert, when a drunk police inspector sits down next to me and starts going on and on about how much he likes me and how he would like us to become engaged as soon as possible. At the same time, he keeps shoving my shoulder with one of his paws, saying, 'Get out of here, get, I don't want anything to do with you, I'm talking to your sister . . .'"

I swallowed this tirade without batting an eye. Hopefully, I managed to remain sufficiently stone-faced.

"Then, as luck would have it," the kid continued, wallowing now. "Up swims a she-Moses to pounce on the inspector for a dance. They muck it up, with me watching, and the place starts to look like a harbor bar in Hamburg. Then he grabs the she-Moses somewhere under her back and drags her behind a curtain, and now it's looking like a completely different type of Hamburg establishment. And there I am staring at the curtain feeling awfully sorry for the inspector, because all things considered he's not a bad guy, he just can't hold his liquor, and there's old Moses also staring predatorily at the very same curtain. Then I get up and ask the she-Moses to dance, which makes the inspector about as happy as can be—apparently he sobered up behind the curtain . . ."

"Who was in the room at that point?" I asked dryly.

"Everyone. Olaf wasn't there, Kaisa wasn't there, Simone was playing pool, feeling sorry that the inspector had stood him up."

"Go on," I said.

"All right, so I'm dancing with the she-Moses, she's pressing herself to me greedily—because who cares, really, so long as I'm not Moses—and then something snaps on her dress. Oh, she says, pardon me, I've had an accident. Well, it's all the same to me, so off she sails with her accident, into the hallway, at which point Olaf swoops down on me . . ."

"Hold on a second—when was that?"

"Come on—why would I have been wearing a watch in there?"

"So Mrs. Moses went out into the hallway?"

"Well, I don't know about the hallway, maybe she went back to her room, or to an empty room—there are two empty ones close by hers . . . Do you want me to go on?"

"Yes."

"So Olaf and I are dancing, he's pouring out various compliments—what a figure, he says, what posture, what a gait . . . and then he says: 'Let's get out of here, I've got something interesting to show you.' And what do I care? All right, let's go . . . I don't see anything else interesting in the room anyway . . ."

"And Mrs. Moses, did you see her in the dining room at this time?"

"No, she was in dry dock, sealing up the crack . . . Well, by now we've made it to the hallway . . . you know the rest."

"And you didn't see Mrs. Moses again?"

I glimpsed a quick hesitation. It was tiny, but I caught it.

"N-no," the child said. "How would I have? I had other things to think about. Like for example drowning my sorrows in vodka."

Its dark glasses were blocking me completely, and I decided firmly that during subsequent interrogations I would take them off. By force, if necessary.

"What were you doing on the roof during the day?" I asked sharply.

"What roof?"

"The roof of the inn," I pointed a finger at the ceiling. "And don't lie, I saw you up there."

"Like hell you did!" The kid bristled. "What do you take me for, some sort of lunatic?"

"Okay, so that wasn't you," I said appeasingly. "Very well. Now, about Hinkus. Remember, he's the little guy, at first you confused him with Olaf . . ."

"I remember," the kid said.

"When was the last time you saw him?"

"The last time? . . . The last time, I guess, was in the hallway, when me and Olaf left the dining room."

I practically jumped out of my seat.

"When?" I asked.

The kid looked alarmed.

"Why?" it asked. "There wasn't anything wrong . . . We'd just made it out of the dining room, I looked—there was Hinkus making his way towards the stairs . . ."

I frantically thought this over. They slipped out of the dining room no earlier than nine o'clock; at nine they were still dancing; Du Barnstoker remembers them being there. But at eight forty-three Hinkus's watch had been crushed, therefore at nine o'clock he was already lying under the table . . .

"Are you sure it was Hinkus?"

The kid shrugged.

"I thought it was Hinkus . . . Then again, he immediately turned left, towards the landing—but still, it was Hinkus, who else would it have been? It's impossible to confuse him with Kaisa or the she-Moses . . . or anyone else. Short, slouching . . ."

"Stop!" I said. "Was he wearing a fur coat?"

"Yes . . . in his stupid toe-length fur coat, with something white on his feet . . . What is this anyway?" The kid switched to a whisper. "He's the murderer, right? Hinkus?"

"No, no," I said. Could Hinkus really have been lying? Was

it a hoax after all? Break the watch, move the hands back . . . and there's Hinkus sitting under the table giggling, and now he's played me and is back in his room still giggling . . . And somewhere his accomplice is giggling too. I jumped up.

"Stay here," I ordered. "Don't you dare leave this room. I'm not finished with you yet."

I went towards the door, then came back and took the bottle from the table.

"I'm confiscating this. I don't need a drunken witness."

"Can I go see my uncle?" the kid said in a trembling voice.

I hesitated for a second, then waved my hand.

"Go on. Maybe he can convince you that it's important to tell the truth."

After dashing into the hallway, I went back to Hinkus's room, unlocked the door and ran inside. All the lights were on: in the entryway, the bathroom, the bedroom. A wet and grinning Hinkus was squatting behind the bed. In the middle of the bed lay a broken chair, and Hinkus was holding one of its legs in his hands.

"Is that you?" he said hoarsely, straightening up.

"Yes!" I said. His appearance, crazy expression and bloodshot eyes again shook my conviction that he was lying and attempting to deceive me. He would have had to be a great artist in order to pull that kind of a role off. Nevertheless, I said sternly, "I'm tired of hearing lies, Hinkus! You're lying to me! You said that they caught you at eight forty. But you were seen in the hallway after nine. Are you going to tell me the truth or not?"

Confusion flashed over his features.

"Me? After nine?"

"Yes! You were in the hallway and stepped on the landing."

"I did?" He suddenly chuckled convulsively. "I was walking in the hallway?" He giggled again, and again, and once more, and suddenly his whole body shook with hysterical laughter. "I? . . . Me? . . . You've got it, Inspector! That's it exactly!" he said, gagging. "I was seen in the hallway . . . and I also saw myself . . . And I grabbed me . . . and tied me up . . . and I bricked myself up in the wall! I—me . . . do you understand, Inspector? I—me!"

10.

I ran into the owner as I was walking down to the lobby.

"Hinkus is completely losing his mind in there," I said grimly. "Do you have any strong sedatives?"

"I have everything," the manager answered, not at all surprised.

"Are you able to give injections?"

"I can do anything."

"Do it," I said, handing him the key.

My head was buzzing. It was five minutes to four. I was tired and worn-out; most importantly, I felt no excitement at being on the trail. I realized all too clearly that this case was beyond my abilities. I hadn't had even the slightest break—on the contrary, the further I went, the worse it got. Maybe there was someone hiding in the inn who looked like Hinkus? Maybe Hinkus really did have a double—a dangerous gangster, maniac and sadist? That would explain some things . . . the murder, Hinkus's fear, his hysteria . . . But then we'd have to solve the problem of how he got here, and where and how he had managed to hide himself. This wasn't exactly the Louvre or the Winter Palace; it was just a "small, cozy inn with twelve rooms, guaranteeing total privacy and all the comforts of home" . . . All right, let's go see the Moseses.

Old Moses didn't let me in his room. He answered my

knock in a long oriental bathrobe, the usual mug in hand, and proceeded to literally push me into the hallway with his fat belly.

"You insist on talking here?" I asked wearily.

"I do," he answered, breathing a complex and unidentifiable mixture of smells into my face. "Right here. A policeman has no business in the Moseses' domicile."

"Then we'd better go to the office," I suggested.

"Wellll . . . The office . . ." He took a sip from his mug. "The office should be fine. Although I don't see what we have to talk about. You suspect me of being a killer, then—me, a Moses?"

"No," I said. "Heaven forbid. But your testimony might provide the investigation with invaluable assistance."

"The investigation!" He snorted disdainfully and took another sip from the mug. "Well, all right, then, let's go . . ." While we were walking, he grunted, "Couldn't find my watch, your run-of-the-mill stolen watch, and now a murder investigation . . ."

In the office, I sat him in the armchair and then sat down at the table.

"So, the watch hasn't been found yet?" I asked.

He eyed me with indignation.

"Is Mr. Police Officer expecting that it will just somehow turn up?"

"I had hopes," I said. "But since it didn't turn up, there's nothing I can do."

"I'm no fan of our police force," Moses said, looking steadily at me. "Or of this inn. Murders, avalanches . . . dogs, thieves, noises in the middle of the night . . . Who did you put in my room? I clearly said that the entire hallway is to be mine, excluding the den. I have no need for a den. How dare you break our agreement? Who is the vagrant they put in room three?"

"He was in the avalanche," I said. "He's been crippled, frostbitten. It would be cruel to have to drag him upstairs."

"But I paid for room three! You were required to ask my permission!"

I couldn't argue with him, I didn't have the strength to explain that his drunk eyes had mistaken me for the owner. So I didn't.

"The management offers its apologies, Mr. Moses, and assures you that tomorrow things will be back to normal."

"Tramps!" Mr. Moses barked, pouncing on his mug. "Is he at least a respectable person, this vagrant in room three? Or is he some sort of thief?"

"An utterly respectable person," I said, attempting to pacify him.

"In that case, why set your repulsive dog to watch him?"

"That is a pure coincidence," I answered, closing my eyes. "Tomorrow things will return to normal, I promise you."

"Perhaps the dead man will be resurrected?" the old bat asked sarcastically. "Perhaps you'd like to promise me that as well? Me, a Moses! Albert Moses, sir! I am not accustomed to dead men, dogs, resurrections, avalanches and cutthroats . . ."

I sat with my eyes closed and waited.

"I am not accustomed to someone bursting in on my wife in the middle of the night," Mr. Moses continued. "I am not accustomed to losing three hundred crowns in one evening to some sort of traveling magician trying to pass himself off as an aristocrat. This Barl . . . Braddle . . . He's simply a hustler! A Moses does not cut cards with hustlers! A Moses—we're talking about a Moses here, sir! . . ."

He babbled on like this, growling, grumbling, slurping noisily, burping and puffing as I internalized the fact that a Moses was a Moses, that this was Albert Moses, sir, that he was not accustomed to this sort of, this damnable snow up to one's knees, but that he was used to such things as, such things as coniferous baths, sir . . . I sat with closed eyes and attempted to escape by imagining how he managed to sleep without letting go of his mug—how he must have balanced it delicately, snoring and whistling, and taking a sip every once in a while, without waking up . . .

"There you have it, Inspector," he said patronizingly, and stood up. "Remember what I said, and let this stand as a lesson to you for the rest of your life. You could learn a lot from it, sir. Good night."

"One minute," I said. "Two small questions." He opened his mouth to voice his dissatisfaction, but I was ready and didn't give him a chance. "Approximately when did you leave the dining room, Mr. Moses?"

"Approximately?" he grunted. "This is how you expect to solve the crime? Approximately! . . . I can give you a precise account. A Moses never does anything approximately, otherwise he wouldn't be a Moses . . . Perhaps I might sit?" he asked sarcastically.

"Yes, I beg your pardon."

"Thank you, Inspector," he said, even more sarcastically, and sat. "So then, I was with Mrs. Moses, whose room you barged into this very night in such an unpleasant manner, without any right, and not alone either, indeed, without even knocking, to say nothing of a warrant or anything of that nature—naturally I have no right to expect today's police to respect such legal niceties as the right that every honest man has to his house, that is to say his fortress, particularly, sir, when we're talking about the wife of a Moses, Albert Moses, Inspector! . . ."

"Yes, yes, that was reckless," I said. "My sincerest apologies to you and Mrs. Moses."

"I am unable to accept your apology, Inspector, until you

clarify for me down to the utmost detail who the person settled in room three is (a room belonging to me), on what basis
he is in a room adjoining my wife's bedroom, and why he is
being guarded by a dog."

"We ourselves are not yet clear down to the utmost detail
as to who this person is," I said, again closing my eyes. "His
car crashed; he is a cripple, he has one arm, he is currently
asleep. As soon as we know anything about who he is, you will
be informed, Mr. Moses." I opened my eyes. "And now, let's go
back to that moment when you and Mrs. Moses left the dining
room. When was that exactly?"

He lifted the mug to his lips and stared balefully at me.

"I am satisfied with your explanation," he declared. "Allow
me to express my hope that you will keep your promise and
report back immediately." He took a sip. "Mrs. Moses and I left
the table and left the room at approximately—" He narrowed
his eyes and with great disdain repeated, "*Approximately*, Inspector, at twenty-one hours and thirty-three minutes local
time. Are you satisfied? Excellent. Let us proceed to your second, and I hope last question."

"We are not yet completely finished with the first one," I
objected. "So, you left the dining room at twenty-one hours
and thirty-three minutes. And then?"

"What 'then'?" Moses asked angrily. "What are you trying
to ask me, young man? You couldn't possibly want to know
what I did when I got back to my room?"

"The investigation would be in your debt, sir," I said
earnestly.

"The investigation? What do I care about your investigation's thanks? Nevertheless, I have nothing to hide. Having
returned to my room, I immediately undressed and went to
bed. I then slept up until the time that awful noise and bustle
arose in room three (which belongs to me). Only my natural

restraint and the consciousness that I was a Moses prevented me from making my way there immediately and dispersing the rabble that the police had gotten together. Keep in mind, however, that my restraint has its limits, I will not tolerate idlers . . ."

"As is your right," I said briskly. "One last question, Mr. Moses."

"The last!" he said, shaking a threatening finger at me.

"Did you notice approximately when Mrs. Moses left the dining room?"

The pause that followed was excruciating. Moses stared at me with bulging eyes, his face turning blue.

"You dare to suggest that the wife of a Moses played a part in the murder?" he said in a choked voice. I shook my head vigorously, but it didn't help. "And you dare suggest that a Moses in that situation would give you any sort of testimony? Or maybe you do not think that you are dealing with a Moses, sir? Perhaps you have allowed yourself to imagine that you are dealing with a one-armed tramp who stole a valuable gold watch from me? Or perhaps . . ."

I closed my eyes. Over the course of the next five minutes, I listened to the most incredible barrage of propositions concerning my intentions and designs, my attack on the honor, dignity, property and even physical security of a Moses, sir, which was not some low dog, good merely as a boarding-house for fleas, but a Moses, Albert Moses, sir—are you capable of understanding that, or not? . . . By the time this speech was drawing to a close, I had already lost hope of receiving any sort of sensible answer. I realized with despair that now I would never get to question Mrs. Moses. But things took an unexpected turn. Suddenly Moses stopped and waited for me to open my eyes, and then said, with indescribable contempt:

"In any event, it's absurd of me to ascribe that kind of

deviousness to such a nonentity. Absurd, and unworthy of a Moses. Naturally, what we have here is a case of simple police bureaucracy and tactlessness, caused by a low level of cultural and intellectual development. I accept your apologies, sir, and give you a farewell salute. In addition, taking the circumstances into consideration . . . I understand that you will not have the decency to leave my wife in peace and spare her from your ridiculous questions. Therefore I give you my permission to ask these questions—no more than two questions, sir! In my presence. Quickly. Follow me."

I followed him, rejoicing inwardly. He knocked on Mrs. Moses's door and, when she answered it, cooed gratingly:

"May I come in, my dear? I am not alone . . ."

My dear, he could. She was lying in the same position under the lamp, now completely dressed. She met us with her charming smile. The old wretch minced his way up to her and kissed her hand—this reminded me for some reason of what the owner had said about his whipping her.

"It's the inspector, my dear," Moses rasped, wilting into the chair. "You remember the inspector?"

"Now how could I forget our dear Inspector Glebsky?" answered the beauty. "Sit down, Inspector, do us the pleasure. A beautiful night, don't you think? So poetical! . . . The moon . . ."

I sat in the chair.

"The inspector has done us the honor," Moses explained, "of making you and me suspects in the murder of that Olaf fellow. You remember Olaf? Well, someone killed him."

"Yes, I heard about that already," Mrs. Moses said. "Terrible. My dear Glebsky, how could you possibly suspect that we'd be involved in such a nightmarish crime?"

All of this was starting to get on my nerves. Enough, I thought. To hell with it.

"Madame," I said dryly. "This investigation has established

that yesterday, at approximately eight thirty in the evening you left the dining room. You can of course confirm this?"

The old man was about to burst out of his armchair, but Mrs. Moses was one step ahead of him.

"I can confirm it, of course," she said. "What reason do I have to deny it? I needed to excuse myself, so I excused myself."

"So far as I can understand it," I continued. "You came here, to your room, and at around nine o'clock you again returned to the dining room. Is this right?"

"Yes, of course. To tell the truth, I can't be certain of the exact time, I didn't look at the clock . . . But most likely it was around then."

"I would like to know if you remember, madame, whether you saw anyone on your trips to and from the dining room."

"Yes, well, let's see . . ." Mrs. Moses said. She furrowed her brow, and I tensed all over. "But of course!" she cried. "When I was on my way back, I saw a couple in the hallway . . ."

"Where?" I asked quickly.

"Well . . . just to the left of the landing. It was our poor Olaf and that amusing little creature . . . I don't know whether to say a boy or a girl . . . Who is he, Moses?"

"One minute," I said. "You are positive that they were standing to the left of the landing?"

"Absolutely positive. They were standing there, holding one another's hands, and cooing quite tenderly. Naturally, I pretended that I hadn't seen anything . . ."

So that's why Brun had hesitated: the kid remembered that someone had seen them outside of Olaf's room, and had had no time to think of an excuse, and so had tried to lie in the hope that nothing would come of it.

"I am a woman, Inspector," Mrs. Moses continued. "And I never interfere in other people's affairs. Under other circumstances, you wouldn't get a peep out of me, but now, it seems that I am obliged to be utterly frank . . . Isn't that right, Moses?"

Moses in his chair muttered something unintelligible.

"Furthermore," Mrs. Moses went on, "but I doubt this is of any special significance . . . On the way down the stairs, I met that unhappy little man . . ."

"Hinkus," I hissed, and coughed. Something had stuck in my throat.

"Yes, Finkus . . . I think that's his name . . . Did you know that he had tuberculosis, Inspector? But you'd never think it, would you?"

"I beg your pardon," I said. "When you met him, was he going up the stairs from the lobby?"

"That should be clear even to a police officer," Moses barked angrily. "My wife told you clearly that she met this Finkus on her way down the stairs. Which means that he must have met her going up . . ."

"Don't be angry, Moses," Mrs. Moses said gently. "The inspector just wants the details. No doubt it is important to him . . . Yes, Inspector, he was walking up the stairs, and, so far as I could tell, from the lobby. He wasn't in a hurry and seemed to be deep in thought, for he didn't pay me a bit of attention. We passed each other and went our separate ways."

"How was he dressed?"

"Awfully! That nightmare of a coat . . . what is it called . . . sheepskin! It even smelled, if you'll excuse me for saying so . . . of wet wool, dog . . . I don't know about you, Inspector, but I think that if a man doesn't have the funds to dress decently he should sit home and try to raise those funds, and not go places where he's likely to run into decent society."

"I would give that advice to many people here," Moses

grumbled over his mug. "Stay home and don't visit places where you're likely to find good society. Well, then, Inspector, are you finally finished?"

"No, not completely," I said slowly. "I have one more question . . . After the ball was over and you went back to your room, I assume, madame, that you went to bed and slept soundly?"

"Slept soundly? . . . Well, how can I put it . . . I napped a little, I was feeling a little excited—no doubt I drank more than I should have . . ."

"But then something must have woken you up," I said. "Because when I broke so awkwardly into your room later that night—I beg your sincere forgiveness—you were not asleep . . ."

"Oh, so that's what you mean . . . Not asleep . . . No, I wasn't asleep, but I can't say, Inspector, that something woke me up. I simply felt that I wouldn't be able to get any good sleep that night, and so decided to read a little. As you can see, I have been reading up to this time . . . Still, if you want to know whether or not I heard any suspicious noises over the course of the night, I can tell you with certainty that I did not."

"No noise at all?" I said, surprised.

She looked at Moses with what seemed to me like confusion. I didn't take my eyes off her.

"So far as I can remember, no," she said, uncertainly. "What about you, Moses?"

"Absolutely not," Moses said definitively. "If you don't consider the blasted fuss raised by these gentlemen over that tramp . . ."

"And neither of you heard the sound of the avalanche? You didn't feel the shock?"

"What avalanche?" a surprised Mrs. Moses said.

"Don't worry, my dear," Moses said. "It's nothing to worry

about. There was an avalanche in the mountains near here, I'll tell you about it afterwards . . . Well, then, Inspector? Perhaps that's enough?"

"Yes," I said. "That's enough." I stood up. "One more, the very last question."

Mr. Moses's growl made him sound just like a riled-up Lel. But Mrs. Moses nodded graciously.

"Go ahead, Inspector."

"This afternoon, shortly before dinner, you, Mrs. Moses, went up on the roof . . ."

She interrupted me with a laugh.

"No, I did not go on the roof. I absentmindedly took the stairs up to the second floor from the lobby and then, without thinking about it, began climbing those awful stairs to the attic. When I suddenly saw the door in front of me, just a few boards really, I felt quite stupid . . . At first, I didn't even realize where I was . . ."

I very much wanted to ask her what she had intended to do on the second floor. I was unable to think what business she might have had up there, though I could assume that it was the rendezvous with Simone which I had interrupted by chance. But at that moment I looked at the old man, and everything else flew out of my head. Because there in Moses's lap lay a whip—a dark black horse-whip with a thick handle and numerous braided tails glistening with metal studs. I averted my eyes in shock.

"Thank you, madame," I muttered. "You have been a great help to this investigation, madame."

Feeling hopelessly tired, I made my way to the lobby and sat down next to the owner to rest. I shook my head, trying to drive out the awful sight of that horse-whip that was still hovering in front of my eyes. It was none of my business. It was a personal matter, of no concern to me . . . My eyes felt

like they'd had sand thrown in them. No doubt I needed to get
some sleep—even just a couple of hours. I still had to question
the stranger, and the kid again, and then interrogate Kaisa, all
of which would take strength, which meant that I had to go to
sleep. But I had the feeling that I wouldn't be able to sleep right
now. Hinkus's doubles were wandering the inn. Du Barnstoker's kid was lying. Not to mention the fact that everything
wasn't exactly right with Mrs. Moses. Either she slept like the
dead, in which case I didn't understand why she'd lied and said
that she barely slept, or she hadn't been sleeping, in which case
I didn't understand why she hadn't heard the avalanche, or the
fracas in the neighboring room. And I absolutely didn't understand what had happened to Simone . . . There were too many
crazies wrapped up in this, I thought dully. Crazies, drunks
and fools . . . But maybe I was going about things the wrong
way? How would Zgut have proceeded in my place? He would
have immediately picked out all those who had the strength to
twist a two-meter-tall Viking's neck and then set to work only
on them. Meanwhile I was wasting my time on a feeble child,
Hinkus the decrepit schizophrenic, Moses, that old alco-
holic . . . No, that wasn't the way to do it. Well, but I might
find the killer. And then what? A typical case of a murder in
a closed room. I would never be able to prove how the killer
came in and how he went out . . . Too bad. Maybe I should get
some coffee . . .

I looked at the owner. He was diligently pressing the adding machine's keys and writing in his account books.

"Listen, Alek," I said. "Is it possible that someone looking
exactly like Hinkus could be hiding undetected in your inn?"

The owner raised his head and looked at me.

"Someone looking exactly like Hinkus?" he said in a businesslike manner. "Not someone else?"

"Yes. An exact double, Alek. Hinkus's double is living in

your inn. He is not paying his bill, Alek. Probably he's been stealing food. Think of it, Alek!"

The owner thought of it.

"I don't know," he said. "I haven't noticed anything like that. To tell you the truth the only thing I feel, Peter, is that you're going about this all wrong. You're following the most natural roads, and for that reason you've ended up in particularly unnatural places. You're exploring alibis, gathering clues, looking for motives. But it seems to me that, in this particular case the usual terms of your art have lost their meaning, the same way that the concept of time changes meaning at speeds faster than light . . ."

"That's your feeling?" I asked bitterly.

"What do you mean?"

"Well, all this speculating about alibis at faster than light speeds. My head starts to feel like a balloon, and god only knows what you're talking about. Better bring me some coffee."

The owner stood up.

"Your understanding of this is still in its infancy, Peter," he said. "I'm waiting for you to finally ripen."

"Why wait for that? I'm ripe enough as it is—I'm practically falling off the branch."

"You aren't going to fall off anything," the owner said soothingly. "Anyway, you've still got some ripening to go. But when you are ripe—when I see that you're ready, then I'll tell you something."

"Tell me now," I said feebly.

"There's no point telling you now. You'd only shake it off and forget it. I want to wait until the moment when it'll be clear that my words are the only thing capable of unlocking this mystery for you."

"Good lord," I muttered. "One can only imagine the truths you've got in store!"

The manager smiled condescendingly and got up to go to the kitchen. On his way out the door he stopped and said:

"If you want, I'll tell you why our great physicist was so surprised?"

"All right, try me," I said.

"When he got in bed with Mrs. Moses, our great physicist found, not a living, breathing, woman, but an unliving, un-breathing mannequin . . . A doll, Peter. Cold as stone."

11.

He stood there, grinning at me from the doorway.

"All right, then, come here," I said. "Tell me."

"What about the coffee?"

"To hell with the coffee! I can see you know something. Don't play games with me, spit it out."

He came back to the table, but didn't sit down.

"I don't know what's going on," he said. "All I can do is draw certain conclusions."

"How did you know what Simone found?"

"Ah! My guess was correct, then . . ." He sat down and made himself comfortable. "Though, to be fair, I could see I'd guessed right by how blown away you looked, Peter. You must agree, that was a pretty effective delivery . . ."

"Listen, Alek," I said. "I like you, I admit it."

"I like you too," he said.

"Shut up. I like you. But that doesn't mean anything. I don't think you're a suspect, Alek. I don't, unfortunately, have any reason to think you're a suspect. But in this regard, you're no different than anyone else . . . I don't have any suspects. But I need one—it's high time for me to start suspecting somebody."

"Try to restrain yourself!" the manager said, lifting a fat finger.

"Didn't I tell you to shut up? Anyway, if you start fooling

with my head, then I'm going to start suspecting you. You'll be in trouble, Alek. I'm very inexperienced when it comes to these sorts of things, which means that you could get in quite a bit of trouble. You have no idea how much trouble an inexperienced policeman can cause a good citizen."

"In that case," he said. "Of course I'll tell you everything. Let's start with how I knew what Mr. Simone saw in Mrs. Moses's bedroom . . ."

"Yes," I said. "How did you know that?"

He sat there in his armchair, broad, heavyset, jovial, unbearably pleased with himself.

"All right, then—let's start with a theory. The witch doctors and folk healers of certain little-known central African tribes have known for some time now how to return their dead fellow-villagers to some semblance of life."

I groaned, and the owner raised his voice:

"This type of real world phenomenon—that is, a dead person who has the appearance of a living one, and who can execute, at first glance, quite rational and independent actions—is called a zombie. Strictly speaking, zombies are not dead . . ."

"Listen, Alek," I said wearily, "none of this interests me. I understand: you're rehearsing the speech you intend to give in front of the newspaper reporters. But none of this interests me in the least! You promised to tell me something concerning Mrs. Moses and Simone. So tell me!"

He stared at me sadly for some time.

"It's true," he said finally. "I thought as much. You're not ripe yet . . . Well, all right, then." He sighed. "Let's put theory aside and look at the facts. Six days ago, when Mr. and Mrs. Moses flattered my inn with a visit, the following event took place. After making all the necessary marks in the passports of the aforementioned gentlefolk, I made my way back to

THE DEAD MOUNTAINEER'S INN   151

Mr. Moses's room with the object of returning their passports to him. I knocked. I was slightly distracted, which is why I opened the door without waiting for permission. My punishment for this transgression against social norms came immediately. In the armchair in the middle of the room I saw something that one might call Mrs. Moses, if they wanted to. But it wasn't Mrs. Moses. It was a large, life-sized, and beautiful doll, which resembled Mrs. Moses very closely and was dressed exactly like her. Now you're going to ask me how I am sure that it was a doll, and not Mrs. Moses. I could list some concrete specifics for you: the unnatural pose, the glassy eyes, the absolute immobility of the features, and so on. But in my opinion this isn't necessary. It seems to me that any normal person is capable of recognizing, in the course of a few seconds, whether he's looking at a model or a mannequin. And I had a few seconds. After which I was rudely grabbed by the shoulder and shoved out into the hallway. That impudent but completely justified action was executed upon my person by Mr. Moses, who'd apparently been looking over his wife's room and attacked me from behind . . .

"A doll . . ." I said pensively.

"A zombie," the owner gently corrected me.

"A doll . . ." I repeated, ignoring him. "What kind of luggage does he have?"

"A couple of the usual suitcases," the owner said. "And this huge, iron-bound, antique wooden trunk. He brought four porters with him, and the poor fellows exhausted themselves trying to get it into the building. They made a wreck of my door post . . ."

"Well, so what?" I said, after I'd thought it over. "At the end of the day, it's his business. I've heard of a millionaire who dragged his collection of chamber pots around with him wherever he went . . . If it pleases a person to have a full-size

mannequin of his spouse . . . no doubt he has time and money
to burn . . . By the way, it's completely possible that he noticed
what our Simone was up to and slipped him the doll instead of
his wife . . . Hell, maybe he carries that doll around with him
just for that purpose! Judging from the behavior of Mrs. Moses . . ." I imagined myself in Simone's place and shuddered.
"Good god, now that's a first-rate joke," I said.

"There you go: now everything's been explained to your
satisfaction," the owner said quietly.

I didn't like his tone. We watched one another for a few
minutes. I still liked him. But damn it all, why did he have to
do this—to clog my brain with all this African nonsense? I
wasn't a reporter, after all, and had no intention of advertising
his establishment to the detriment of my own reputation . . .
No, I'd had enough. I was done talking with Mr. Alek Snevar
about these things. If he wanted to throw me off the scent,
he wasn't going to succeed. He was only making his situation
worse. He didn't want me paying that much attention to him.

"Look, Alek," I said. "You're messing me up. Sit here for
a while; I'm going to go to the den. I have to think this over."

"It's quarter to five," the owner reminded me.

"So what? We're not sleeping today anyway. Keep in mind,
Alek, I don't think this is over yet. So stay here in the hallway
and be ready."

"All right. I suppose you've got to do what you've got to
do," the owner said.

I went into the den (Lel snarled at me again), picked up
the poker and proceeded to jumble the embers. So, the in-
cident with Simone had been more or less explained, and I
could put it out of my head. Or was it the other way around,
since if that had been a doll in the Mrs. Moses's room at eleven
o'clock, then where had Mrs. Moses been? A first-rate joke, of
course . . . But there was something too cumbersome about

it . . . Was it really a joke? Maybe an attempt to establish an alibi? . . . Not much of an alibi: it was night, dark, the only way anyone would have known it was her was by touch, and with touch it turned into a joke, not an alibi. Maybe what they were thinking was that poor Simone's nerves would snap, he'd yell out in horror, get to his feet, stir up a scandal, a hullabaloo . . . and then what? Most importantly, what did the doll have to do with it? All this could have been done without the doll. So what, essentially, was bothering me about it? Only one thing: that Simone's room was located next to Olaf's. This allowed one to suppose, say, that the Moseses needed Simone's room to be empty for a span of time after eleven o'clock. That's what was bothering me. But they wouldn't have needed a doll to distract Mr. Simone. Of course, hypothetically speaking, the doll could have caused Simone to fall into a long and deep faint . . . but then, to distract Simone, all you needed was Mrs. Moses. That would have been the most natural way, and the one with the greatest hope of succeeding. The only reason to resort to such an unnatural and unreliable method as a doll would be if Mrs. Moses had to be somewhere else. Mrs. Moses . . . a fragile socialite, pampered to the point of imbecility . . . No, this wasn't getting me anywhere. It could still have just been a first-rate joke, after all, though I didn't see how this story fit yet . . .

It was a particularly sticky situation. None of the strands led anywhere. First, there wasn't a single suspect. Second, I had absolutely no idea how the crime had been committed. I didn't understand the most important thing. Forget about the killer—how had it been done? How? An open window, but no traces on the sill, no footprints in the snow on the ledge. No way to approach the window from below, the right, or the left. That left only one way: from above. From the roof, using a rope. But then there would be traces on the edge of the roof. Of course I could go back up and examine it again, but I remembered it exactly: the snow had been disturbed only around Hinkus's lounge chair. Of course there was always the possibility that the killer had stuck a propeller in his ass like Karlsson-on-the-Roof. He took off, snapped his countryman's neck, flew away . . . So I had only two lousy possibilities. The first were secret passages, hidden doorways and double walls. And the second was that some genius had invented a new technological device that allowed one to turn a key from the outside, leaving no trace behind . . .

Both propositions led, among other places, directly to the owner of the house and a mechanical inventor. Well, all right. And how does this man's alibi look to us? Until nine thirty he'd been sitting continuously at the card table. From five to ten until the moment the body was discovered, he had been either where I could see him or within earshot. That left only twenty to twenty-five minutes for him to commit the murder, during which he either hadn't been seen, or had been seen only by Kaisa, who, according to his own testimony, he'd been yelling at. Hence he could, theoretically, be the killer, if he knew of a secret passageway or had the means to turn a key from the outside without leaving any trace behind . . . I couldn't understand what the motive behind all this completely psychologically unjustified behavior might be (definitely not publicity!), but, I repeat, theoretically he could have been the murderer. Let's make a note of this and move on.

Du Barnstoker. He didn't have an alibi. But he's a weak old man, he doesn't have the strength to break a man's neck . . . Simone. He didn't have an alibi. He could break a man's neck—he's a strong fellow, not to mention a little off-kilter. I couldn't work out how he might have gotten into Olaf's room. And if he did get in, I couldn't understand how he got out. Theoretically (of course) he might have stumbled accidentally over the alleged secret door. I didn't understand his motives, didn't understand his behavior after the murder. I didn't understand anything . . . Hinkus . . . Hinkus's double . . . Another cup of coffee would be nice. Then again, it'd be nice to spit on it all and go to bed . . .

Brun. Yes, here was one thread that hadn't snapped yet. That child had lied to me. The child had seen Mrs. Moses, but had said that it hadn't seen her. The child had been canoodling with Olaf at the door to his room, but had stated that it slapped him by the dining-room doors . . . And then suddenly I remembered. I'd been sitting here, in this chair. The floor had shaken, I'd heard the hum of the avalanche. I looked at the clock, it had been two minutes after ten, and then upstairs a door slammed loudly. One flight up. Someone had slammed that door—hard. Who? Simone was shaving at the time. Du Barnstoker was sleeping and, possibly, had just been woken up by the same sound. Hinkus was lying tied up under the table. The owner and Kaisa were in the kitchen. The Moses-es were in their rooms. That meant that the door could only have been slammed by either Olaf, or Brun, or the murderer. Hinkus's double, for example . . . I threw the poker down and ran upstairs.

The kid's room was empty, so I knocked on Du Barnstoker's door. The kid was sitting gloomily at the table, its cheeks propped on its fists. A tartan-wrapped Du Barnstoker was dozing in a chair by the window. Both of them practically jumped when I came in.

"Take your glasses off!" I ordered sharply, and the kid immediately obeyed.

Yes: a girl. A very pretty one, although her eyes were red and swollen from tears. Stifling a sigh of relief, I sat down opposite her and said,

"Listen, Brun. Stop withholding information. You

personally are not in any danger. I don't think you're the murderer, so you have nothing to gain by lying. At nine ten, Mrs. Moses saw you and Olaf here . . . in the hallway, outside the door to his room. You lied to me. You and Olaf didn't go your separate ways at the doors to the dining room. So where did you leave him? Where, when, and under what circumstances?"

She looked at me for some time, her lips trembling, her red eyes again filling up with tears. Then she covered her face with her hands.

"We were in his room," she said.

Du Barnstoker moaned piteously.

"Don't moan, uncle!" Brun said, immediately flaring up. "Nothing irreparable happened. We kissed, and it was pretty fun, only cold because his window was open the whole time. I don't remember how long it lasted. I remember he pulled something that looked like a necklace out of his pocket—beads or something—and wanted to put it around my neck, but then there was a roar and I said, 'Listen: an avalanche!' and he suddenly let go of me and held his head as if he'd remembered something . . . You know how people hold their heads when they remember something important . . . It lasted a few seconds. He rushed to the window, but then came right back, grabbed my shoulders and literally threw me out into the hallway. I almost fell down, and he slammed the door immediately behind me. He didn't even say anything, he just swore under his breath, and I remember that he turned the key in the door, too. I didn't see him again. I was crazy with anger because he'd acted like a pig, he even swore at me, so I immediately went back to my room and got drunk . . ."

Du Barnstoker groaned again.

"All right," I said. "He held his head as if he'd remembered something, and rushed to the window . . . Maybe someone called out to him?"

Brun shook her head.

"No. I didn't hear anything, only the sound of the avalanche."

"And you left immediately? You didn't linger outside the door for a second?"

"Immediately. I was going crazy."

"Good. And what happened after you and he left the dining room? Tell me again."

"He said that he wanted to show me something," she said, bowing her head. "We went into the hallway, and he began leading me to his room. I resisted, of course . . . but, you know, we were joking around. Afterwards, when we were already standing outside his door . . ."

"Stop. Before you said you saw Hinkus."

"Yes, we saw him. As soon as we went into the hallway. He was turning from the hallway onto the stairs."

"Right. Go on."

"While we were standing outside Olaf's door, the Moses woman showed up. Naturally, she pretended that she hadn't seen us, but I was embarrassed . . . It's annoying when people dawdle around and stare at you. Anyway . . . after that we made our way to Olaf's room . . ."

"I understand." I looked at Barnstoker. The old man was sitting, his eyes raised grievously towards the ceiling. It served him right. Uncles like him always imagine that they're sheltering angels under their wings. Meanwhile those angels are making counterfeit bills. "Okay. You drank something at Olaf's?"

"Me?"

"I'm interested in what Olaf drank."

"Nothing. We didn't drink, neither of us."

"Now . . . hm . . . Did you notice . . . m-hm . . . Did you notice any strange smell?"

"No. The air in there was very clear and fresh."

"I'm not talking about the room, dammit. When you kissed, did you notice anything strange? A strange smell is what I mean . . ."

"I didn't notice anything," Brun said angrily.

For a few moments I tried to think of a way to put my next question delicately, then I gave up and asked directly.

"There is the possibility that Olaf might have been given a slow-acting poison before being murdered. You didn't notice anything that would confirm this possibility?"

"And what would I have noticed?"

"You can usually tell when someone feels sick," I clarified. "Especially when someone is getting sicker and sicker before your eyes."

"There was nothing like that," Brun said decisively. "He was feeling great."

"You didn't turn the light on?"

"No."

"And you don't remember anything he said that sounded strange?"

"I don't remember a thing he said," Brun said quietly. "It was the usual patter. Jokes, one-liners, flirting . . . We talked about motorcycles, and skiing. He seemed like a pretty good mechanic. He knew his way around all sorts of engines . . ."

"And he didn't show you anything interesting? After all, he said he wanted to show you something . . ."

"Of course not. Don't you get it? He just said that . . . well, to say something . . ."

"When the avalanche happened, were you sitting down or standing up?"

"We were standing up."

"Where?"

"Right by the door. I was already bored and was getting

ready to leave. And then he started to try and put the necklace on me . . ."

"And you're sure that he ran from you to the window?"

"How am I supposed to . . . He grabbed his head, turned his back to me, made a step or two towards the window . . . In the direction of the window . . . Well, I don't know how else to put it, maybe not to the window, of course, but I just didn't see anything else in the room other than the window . . ."

"Do you think that there could have been anyone else in the room other than you? Maybe now you remember some noises, strange sounds that you didn't pay attention to at the time . . ."

She thought about this.

"No, it was quiet . . . There were a few noises, but on the other side of the wall. Olaf made a joke that Simone was in his room walking up the walls . . . But there wasn't anything else."

"And was the noise really coming from Simone's room?"

"Yes," Brun said confidently. "We were standing already, and the noise was coming from my left. Anyway, it was just normal noises. Steps, water from the faucet . . ."

"Olaf moved some furniture around while you were there?"

"Furniture? . . . Yes, he did actually. He said he wouldn't let me out, and pulled a chair over to the door . . . Afterwards he pushed it out of the way, of course . . ."

I stood up.

"That's all for now," I said. "Go to bed. I won't bother you again today."

Du Barnstoker stood up too and moved towards me with outstretched arms.

"My dear inspector! You understand of course that I had no idea . . ."

"Yes, Du Barnstoker," I said. "But children grow up. All

children. Even children whose parents have died. From this point on, don't let her wear dark glasses. The eyes are the mirrors to the soul."

I left them to reflect on these nuggets of inspectorial wisdom, and went down the hallway.

"You've been rehabilitated, Alek," I announced to the owner.

"I had no idea I'd been convicted," he said, looking up with surprise from his adding machine.

"What I mean to say is that I've taken all suspicion off you. You have an airtight alibi now. But don't think that gives you the right to clog my head with all your zombie mumbo-jumbo . . . Don't interrupt me. Right now you're going to stay here and remained seated until I permit you to get up. Don't forget that I have to be the first person to talk to the one-armed fellow."

"And if he wakes up before you do?"

"I am not going to sleep," I said. "I want to search the building. If that poor sap wakes up and calls for anyone, even his mother, get me immediately."

"Yes, sir," said the owner. "One question. Is the inn's schedule to remain the same as before?"

I thought about this.

"I suppose so. Breakfast at nine. And then we'll see . . . By the way, Alek, when in your opinion should we expect anyone from Mur to arrive here?"

"Hard to say. The excavation of the avalanche could begin as early as tomorrow. I remember times when things have happened this efficiently . . . But then again, they know full well that we're not in any danger here . . . It's possible that in two days Tsvirik the mountain inspector will arrive by helicopter . . . If the other locations are doing all right. The whole problem is that first they need to hear about the avalanche somewhere . . . In short, I wouldn't count on anything happening tomorrow . . ."

"You mean today?"

"Yes, today . . . But tomorrow someone could fly in."

"You don't have a radio transmitter?"

"Where would I get one? And more importantly, why would I have one? It's not worth the cost for me, Peter."

"I understand," I said. "Tomorrow, then . . ."

"I won't say tomorrow definitely either," the manager said.

"Then in the next two or three days . . . All right. Now, Alek—suppose you wanted to hide in this building. For a long time, several days. Where would you hide?"

"Hm . . ." the manager said skeptically. "You still think that there's an outsider in the inn?"

"Where would you hide?" I repeated.

The manager shook his head.

"You're barking up the wrong tree," he said. "Honestly. There's nowhere to hide here. Twelve rooms, only two of which are empty—but Kaisa cleans them every day, she would have noticed something. People always leave trash behind them, and she's a stickler for cleanliness . . . As for the basement, I locked it from the outside, with a padlock . . . There isn't any attic, in the space between the roof and the ceiling there's barely room for your hand . . . The service rooms are all locked from the outside too, and anyway, we spend all day running around there, sometimes me, sometimes Kaisa. And that's everything."

"How about the upstairs shower?" I asked.

"Good point. There is an upstairs shower, and we haven't checked it in a long time. Also, it might be worth looking at the generator room—I don't look around there that much either. Go look, Peter, snoop around . . ."

"Give me the keys," I said.

I looked and I snooped. I clambered around in the basement, peeked into the shower, examined the garage, the boiler room, the generator room—I even took a look at the underground oil tank. Nothing. Naturally, I hadn't expected to discover anything, that would have been too simple, but my damned bureaucratic integrity wouldn't let me leave any stone unturned. Twenty years of impeccable service are twenty years of impeccable service; anyway, it's always better to look like a scrupulous blockhead rather than the slapdash man of talent in the eyes of one's superiors, not to mention subordinates. So I groped, crawled, wallowed, breathing in dust and trash, pitying myself and cursing my stupid fate.

When I made my way out of the underground tanks, upset and filthy, it was already dawn. The pale moon was leaning to the west. The huge grey cliffs were covered in a purple mist. And what fresh, sweet, frosty air had filled the valley! Damn it all! . . .

I had just made it back to the inn when the door swung open and the owner came out onto the porch.

"Aha," he said, catching sight of me. "I was just going to get you. Our poor man woke up and is asking for his mother."

"I'm coming," I said, shaking my jacket off.

"Just kidding," the manager said. "He didn't ask for his mother—he asked for Olaf Andvarafors."

12.

When he caught sight of me, the stranger leaned forward eagerly and asked, "Are you Olaf Andvarafors?"

I wasn't expecting this question. I wasn't expecting it at all. I looked around for a chair, pulled one up to the side of the bed, sat down slowly and only then looked at the stranger. I was very tempted to answer in the affirmative and see what happened. But I am not a detective and not in counter-intelligence. I'm an honest police bureaucrat. So instead I answered:

"No. I am not Olaf Andvarafors. I am a police inspector, and my name is Peter Glebsky."

"Really?" he said, surprised but unruffled. "But where's Olaf Andvarafors?"

Apparently he had recovered completely from yesterday's events. His thin face had become rosy; the tip of his long nose, which had been so white last night, was now red. He sat on the bed, a blanket pulled up to his waist. The neck of Alek's nightshirt (which was clearly too big for him) hung open, revealing his sharp collarbone and the pale hairless skin of his chest. His face was hairless too—only a few whiskers where his eyebrows should be and sparse white eyelashes. He sat, leaning forward, his left hand absentmindedly gathering up his empty right sleeve.

"I'm sorry," I said. "But first I have to ask you a few questions."

The stranger didn't say anything to this. His face took on a strange expression—so strange that at first I didn't understand what was happening. But then I realized that one of his eyes was fixed on me, while the other eye had rolled up in its socket, so that I could barely see it. Some time passed in silence.

"Well, then," I said. "Before anything else I would like to know who you are and what your name is."

"Luarvik," he said quickly.

"Luarvik . . . And your first name?"

"First name? Luarvik."

"Mr. Luarvik Luarvik?"

He was quiet again. I struggled with the feeling of discomfort that one always gets when dealing with very cross-eyed people.

"More or less, yes," he said finally.

"What do you mean 'more or less'?"

"Luarvik Luarvik."

"Very well. If you say so. Who are you?"

"Luarvik," he said. "I am Luarvik." He was quiet. "Luarvik Luarvik. Luarvik L. Luarvik."

He looked healthy enough, and, what was more surprising, completely serious. But I'm not a doctor.

"I would like to know your occupation."

"I'm mechanic," he said. "Mechanic and driver."

"A driver of what?" I asked.

Here he stared at me with both his eyes. He clearly did not understand the question.

"All right, we'll put that aside for now," I said quickly. "You're a foreigner?"

"Very much," he said. "For the most part."

"A Swede, most likely?"

"Most likely. A Swede, for the most part."

Was he mocking me, I wondered? Probably not. He looked like a man with his back up against the wall.

"Why did you come here?" I asked.

"Olaf Advarafors is here. He will tell you everything. I can't."

"You were coming to see Olaf Andvarafors?"

"Yes."

"You were caught under the avalanche?"

"Yes."

"You were traveling by car?"

He thought about this.

"By car," he said.

"Why do you need to see Andvarafors?"

"I have business."

"What kind of business exactly?"

"I have business," he repeated. "With him. He will tell you."

The door creaked behind my back. I turned around. On the doorstep, holding his mug at arm's length, was Moses.

"You're not allowed in here," I said sharply.

Moses stared at the stranger from underneath his bushy eyebrows. He wasn't paying any attention to me. I jumped out of my seat and walked directly up to him.

"I am asking you to leave immediately, Mr. Moses!"

"Don't scream at me," he said in an unexpectedly pacific voice. "Can't I inquire about whom you have put in my room?"

"Not now. Later . . ." Gradually, but forcefully, I managed to close the door.

"All right, all right," Moses muttered, as he was pushed into the hallway. "I could object, of course . . ."

I closed the door and turned again to Luarvik L. Luarvik.

"Was that Olaf Andvarafors?" Luarvik asked.

"No," I said. "Olaf Andvarafors was killed last night."

"Killed," Luarvik repeated. There was no emotion in his voice. No surprise, no fear, no grief. It was as if I had told him that Olaf had just stepped out and would be back in a minute. "He's dead? Olaf Andvarafors?"

"Yes."

"No," said Luarvik. "Your information is inaccurate."

"My information is completely accurate. I saw his body myself."

"I would like to see."

"Why do you want to see it? So far as I understand it, you did not know him personally."

"I have business," said Luarvik.

"But I am telling you: he has been killed. He is dead. Someone murdered him."

"Fine. I would like to see."

Suddenly I remembered: the suitcase.

"Was he supposed to give you something?"

"No," he answered indifferently. "We were supposed to talk. He and I."

"About what?"

"He and I. Me and him."

"Listen, Mr. Luarvik," I said. "Olaf Andvarafors is dead. He has been murdered. I am investigating his murder. I am looking for the murderer. Do you understand? I need to know as much as possible about Olaf Andvarafors. I am asking you to be candid about this. Sooner or later you are going to have to tell me everything. Better sooner than later."

Suddenly he pulled the blanket up to his nose. His eyes drifted apart again.

"I can't tell you anything," he said. His voice was muffled by the blanket.

"Why not?"

"I can only tell Olaf Andvarafors."

"Where are you coming from?" I asked.

He was quiet.

"Where do you live?"

Silence. Quiet sniffling. One eye looked at me, the other at the ceiling.

"Are you following orders?"

"Yes."

"Whose, exactly?"

"Why do you want to know this?" he asked. "My business isn't with you. Your business isn't with us."

"I am asking you to understand," I said earnestly. "If we find out something about Olaf, we will be able to find out who his murderer is. Granted, you apparently don't know Olaf. But whoever sent you to him, they might know something."

"They also do not know Olaf," he said.

"What do you mean?"

"They don't know Olaf. What do *you* mean?"

I rubbed the stubble of my unshaven cheeks.

"You're not making any sense," I said gloomily. "Some people who don't know Olaf sent you, who also doesn't know Olaf, with some sort of business for Olaf. How is this possible?"

"It's possible. It is."

"Who are these people?"

Silence.

"Where are they?"

Silence.

"Mr. Luarvik, you may be in big trouble."

"Why?" he asked.

"When a murder is being investigated, good citizens have a responsibility to provide the police with the desired information," I said strictly. "Failure to do so could be seen as complicity."

Luarvik L. Luarvik did not react to this.

"It is not impossible that you might be arrested," I added. It was clearly illegal to threaten him this way, and I hurried to add, "In any event, your stubborn resistance will hurt you a great deal during the trial."

"I would like to wear clothes," Luarvik said suddenly. "I do not want to lie here. I want to see Olaf Andvarafors."

"For what reason?" I asked.

"I want to see him."

"But you don't know what he looks like."

"I don't care what he looks like," Luarvik said.

"Then what do you want with him?"

Luarvik crawled out from under the blanket and sat up again.

"I want to see Olaf Andvarafors!" he said very loudly. His right eye was twitching and rotating. "Why all these questions? Why more questions? So many questions. Why don't I see Olaf Andvarafors?"

I was losing patience too.

"You want to identify the body? Is that how I'm supposed to understand you?'

"Identify . . . You mean recognize him?"

"Yes! Recognize him!"

"Yes. I want to see him."

"How do you expect to recognize him," I said, "if you don't know what he looks like?"

"What do you mean what he looks like?" Luarvik yelled. "Why do you ask me what he looks like? I want to make sure this is not Olaf Andvarafors, that it is someone else!"

"Why do you think that it's someone else?" I asked him quickly.

"Why do you think that it's Olaf Andvarafors?" he answered.

We stared at each other. I had to admit, this strange person had a point. I couldn't have sworn that this Viking with his twisted neck was the same Olaf Andvarafors as the one that Luarvik L. Luarvik was looking for. It might not be that Olaf Andvarafors—it might not be Olaf Andvarafors at all. On the other hand, I did not understand what sense there was in showing Olaf's body to someone who didn't know what he looked like. Face to face . . . But then come to think of it, what was so important about the face? Maybe he had to be recognized by his clothes, or a signet ring, or let's say a tattoo . . .

There was a knock at the door, and Kaisa's voice squeaked, "Clothes, sir . . ." I opened the door and took the stranger's dried and ironed suit from Kaisa.

"Get dressed," I said, laying the suit on the bed.

I walked over to the window and proceeded to look out on the Dead Mountaineer's toothy cliffs, already lit with the rosy light of the rising sun; on the pale dot of the moon; on the clear blue sky. Behind me there was rustling, mumbling, scraping; for some reason a chair was being moved (apparently, it was not so easy to get dressed with both one arm and a squint). Twice I felt the urge to turn around and offer some help, but I held myself back. Then Luarvik said, "Dressed."

I turned around. I was surprised. I was very surprised, but then I remembered what this man had lived through overnight, and stopped being surprised. I walked up to him, straightened and buttoned his collar, rebuttoned his jacket, and slid the manager's slippers over to him. While I was doing all this he stood there submissively, holding out his lone hand. The empty right sleeve I put in his pocket. He looked at the slippers and said doubtfully:

"These aren't mine. I don't have ones like these."

"Your shoes haven't dried yet," I said. "Put them on, let's go."

You would have thought he'd never seen a pair of slippers before in his life. He tried twice, and failed twice, to drive his feet into them with a sweeping motion, losing his balance each time. His equilibrium seemed off in general—clearly he'd been through a lot, and wasn't yet himself. I understood this well: I'd had similar experiences myself . . .

Some kind of machine must have been spinning away silently in my subconscious, because suddenly I was struck by a wonderful idea: what if Olaf wasn't Olaf, but Hinkus, and Hinkus wasn't Hinkus, but Olaf? What if he'd summoned this strange man via telegram? But nothing came of this transmutation of names, and I shook the thought out of my head.

Hand in hand we went out into the hall and up to the second floor. The owner, who was sitting at his post as he had been earlier, gave us a thoughtful look. Luarvik didn't pay him any attention. He was focused completely on the stairs. I held on to his elbow just to be careful.

We stopped in front of the door to Olaf's room. I carefully inspected the tape I'd put up: it was all in order. Then I took out the key and opened the door. A sharp unpleasant odor struck my nose—a very strange odor, not unlike the smell of disinfectant. I lingered in the doorway, trying to pull myself together. But everything in the room was just as it had been. Only, the face of the dead man seemed darker to me than it had the night before, possibly because of the lighting, and I could barely see the bruises anymore. Luarvik was nudging me insistently between the shoulder blades. I walked into the entryway and stepped aside so that he could see.

He might have been a mortician, instead of a mechanic and driver. He stood over the body with a completely indifferent look on his face; he bent low, placing his single hand behind his back. There was no disgust, no fear, no awe: this was just a businesslike inspection. Strangest of all was what he said next.

"I'm surprised," he said in an utterly flat tone. "This really is Olaf Andvarafors. I don't understand."

"How did you recognize him?" I asked immediately.

Still bending over, he turned his head and looked at me with one eye.

He was standing there bent, with his feet far apart, looking up at me quietly.

This lasted so long that my neck began to hurt. How could he remain in that ridiculous position? Was he having lower back problems, or what? Finally he said:

"I remembered. I've seen him before. At that time, I did not know it was Olaf Andvarafors."

"And where did you see him before?" I asked.

"There." Still bent over, he waved a hand towards the window. "It's not important."

Suddenly he straightened up and lurched around the room, turning his head in a funny way. I braced myself, never taking my eyes off him. He was clearly looking for something, and I had already guessed what that something was . . .

"Olaf Andvarafors did not die here?" he asked, stopping in front of me.

"Why do you think that?" I asked.

"I don't think. I asked."

"Are you looking for something?"

"Olaf Andvarafors had one object with him," he said. "Where it is?"

"You're looking for his suitcase?" I asked. "You came here for it?"

"Where it is?" Luarvik repeated.

"I have it," I said.

"Good," he said. "I would like to have. Bring, please."

I ignored his tone and said.

"I could bring you the suitcase, but first you have to answer my questions."

"Why?" he said in amazement. "Why more questions?"

"Because," I said patiently. "You will receive the suitcase only if your answers to my questions demonstrate that you have the right to it."

"I don't understand," he said.

"I don't know," I said. "Whether it's your suitcase or not. If it's yours, if Olaf brought it here for you, then prove it. Then I'll give it to you."

His eyes drifted apart and then focused again on the bridge of his nose.

"Don't," he said. "I don't want to. I'm tired. Let's go."

I followed him out of the room feeling a little puzzled. The air in the hallway seemed surprisingly clean and fresh. Where had that apothecary's stench in the room come from? Perhaps something had been spilled in there earlier, but the window being opened had masked the smell? I closed the door. Luarvik remained where he was, apparently immersed in deep thought, as I got the glue and paper from my room and set to work resealing the scene.

"So what's it going to be?" I asked. "Are you going to answer my questions?"

"No," he said decisively. "I don't want questions. I want to lie down. Where can I lie down?"

"Go back to your room," I said numbly. I was overcome with apathy. Suddenly I had a splitting headache. I wanted to relax, lie down, close my eyes. The entire absurd, unprecedented, messed-up, nonsensical case seemed to be coming to life in the form of the absurd, unprecedented, messed-up, nonsensical Luarvik L. Luarvik.

We went down the hall; he staggered back to his room, and

I sat in the armchair, stretched myself out and, finally, closed my eyes. Somewhere I could hear the sea murmuring, loud, insensible music, dark spots swimming towards me and away from me. My mouth felt like I'd been chewing for hours on a damp rag. Then I felt a wet nose sniff my ear, and Lel's heavy head leaned consolingly against my knee.

13.

I managed to nap for about fifteen minutes before Lel intervened. He licked my ears and cheeks, tugged at my pant legs, jostled and then, finally, lightly bit my hand. At this point, I couldn't hold back anymore; I jumped up, ready to tear him to pieces, incoherent curses and complaints stuck in my throat, but then my gaze fell on the side table and I froze. On its shiny lacquer top, next to the owner's papers and receipts, lay a large black pistol.

It was a .45-caliber Luger with an extended handle. It was lying in a little puddle of water, and there were still clumps of unmelted snow sticking to it; with my mouth hanging open I watched one of these lumps drip down the trigger and onto the tabletop. I looked around the lobby. The only one there was Lel, standing beside the table. He tipped his head to the side, giving me a stern and curious look.

Normal kitchen-type noises were coming out of the kitchen, the owner's soft bass could be heard and there was a drifting smell of coffee.

"Did you bring me this?" I asked Lel with a whisper.

He tipped his head to the other side and continued to look at me. His paws were covered in snow, and his shaggy belly was still dripping. I picked the pistol up carefully.

It was a true gangster's weapon. Its effective range was

two hundred meters; it had a place to put a sight, a switch for automatic firing, and other amenities. The barrel was full of snow. The gun was cold, heavy; its ribbed handle lay comfortably in my palm. For some reason I remembered that I hadn't searched Hinkus. I'd searched his luggage, his coat, but I'd forgotten to search his person. Probably because I'd thought he was a victim.

I pulled the clip out of the handle: it was full. I pulled back the bolt and a bullet jumped out onto the table. I picked it up to put it back in the clip, but was arrested suddenly by the strange color of the bullet. It was not the usual dull gray or yellow. It was shiny, like it was nickel-plated, but it looked more silver than nickel. I had never seen a bullet like it before in my life. One after another I hurriedly expelled the bullets from the cartridge. All of them were the same silvery color. I licked my dry lips and looked at Lel again.

"Where'd you get this, old man?" I asked.

Lel playfully shook his head and leapt sideways to the door.

"I get it," I said. "I understand. Wait a minute."

I put the bullets back into the clip, drove the clip into the handle and shoved the pistol in a side pocket on my way to the door. Outside, Lel rolled off the porch and, falling into the snow, galloped along the facade. I felt almost certain that he was going to stop beneath Olaf's window—but he didn't. He circled the house, disappearing for a second and then reappearing again to peer eagerly at me from around the corner. I grabbed the first pair of available skis, fastened them haphazardly on my feet and immediately ski'd after him.

After we had circled the inn Lel shot off, stopping about fifty meters away from the building. I made my way to him and looked around. All of this was strange. I saw a hole in the snow, from which Lel had dug up the pistol; I saw the tracks of my skis behind me; I saw the furrows that Lel had made jumping through the snowbanks; but the rest of the ground around us was unmarked. This could only mean one thing: the pistol had been thrown here, from either the road or the inn. Either way, it was a good throw. I wasn't sure that I would have been able to heave such a heavy and unwieldy thing so far. Then I understood. The pistol had been thrown from the roof. They'd taken the gun from Hinkus and thrown it away. Or else, maybe Hinkus had thrown the gun away himself. Maybe he had been afraid of being caught with the gun. Or maybe Hinkus himself hadn't done it, but someone else . . . anyway, it definitely had to be from the roof. Only an exceptional arm could have thrown that far from the road, and to do it from any of the rooms would have been completely impossible.

"Well, Lel," I said to the Saint Bernard, "you've done a good job. Better than me. I should have shaken down Hinkus more thoroughly, the way old Zgut would have done it. Right? Luckily it's not too late."

I set off back to the inn without waiting for Lel's response. He galloped along beside me, scattering snow, falling through drifts and swinging his ears.

I intended to find Hinkus immediately—to wake that son of a bitch up and shake him to within an inch of his life, even if it cost me a reprimand on my end of year review. It was clear to me now that the cases of Olaf and Hinkus were connected in the most direct way; that their arrival here together hadn't been an accident; that Hinkus had been sitting on the roof armed with a long-range pistol and a single purpose: to keep a close watch on the immediate surroundings and not let anyone leave the inn; that he was the one who had sent the note as a warning, signing it "F" (he'd sent it to the wrong room, of course: Du Barnstoker couldn't possibly be wrapped up in this), that his presence here had caused and was still causing someone great difficulties, and that I'd be damned if I wasn't going to find out right now who that someone was, and why it was happening. There were a lot of contradictions to this version of things, of course. Let's say Hinkus was Olaf's bodyguard, and was thwarting his murderer—well, then, why had they dealt with Hinkus himself so lightly? Why hadn't they broken his neck too? Why had his enemy deployed such an exceptionally humane tactic as capturing him and tying him up? Actually, this would have been easy to explain: Hinkus was clearly a hired man, and they just didn't want to get their hands dirty with him . . . Yes! I had to find out who he'd sent that telegram to . . . I'd forgotten about this the whole time . . .

The owner called out to me from the pantry and, without saying another word, offered me a mug of hot coffee and a huge sandwich triangle with fresh ham. It was exactly what I needed. He looked at me as I chewed rapidly, and then finally asked:

"Anything new?"

I nodded.

"Yes. A pistol. Only I didn't find it—Lel did. Also, I'm an idiot."

"Hm . . . Yes. Lel's a smart dog. What kind of pistol?"

"An interesting one," I said. "Professional . . . By the way, have you ever heard of a gun being loaded with silver bullets?"

The owner was quiet for a while, his jaw bulging.

"Your gun is loaded with silver bullets?" he said slowly.

I nodded.

"Hmm . . . well, I've read about it," the owner said. "People load their weapons with silver bullets when they're planning to shoot ghosts."

"More zombie mumbo-jumbo," I grumbled. But then I remembered hearing about this myself.

"Yes, more. Normal bullets won't kill ghouls. Werewolves, kitsune foxes . . . frog queens . . . I warned you, Peter!" He raised a fat finger. "I've been waiting for something like this for a long time. And now it turns out I'm not the only one . . ."

I finished chewing my sandwich and drank the rest of my coffee. I can't say that the owner's words didn't give me pause. For whatever reason, it appeared that the single fantastic version of the events that he'd offered was constantly being confirmed, while my many realistic ones were not . . . Ghouls, phantoms, ghosts . . . The only problem was that, if this was the case then there was nothing left for me to do but turn in my weapon: as some writer or another said, the afterlife is the church's business, not the police's . . .

"Have you figured out whose gun it is?" the manager asked.

"Yes, we have one ghoul hunter here—a certain Hinkus," I said and left.

Standing in the middle of the lobby, looking very awkward and unnatural, like a stuffed doll, was Mr. Luarvik L. Luarvik. He stared at me with one eye, as the other peered up the stairs. His jacket looked particularly crooked on him, his pants were slipping down, his dangling empty sleeve looked like a cow had been chewing on it. I nodded and tried to walk past him, but he quickly hobbled forward to stand directly in my way.

"Yes?" I said, stopping short.

"A small but important conversation," he announced.

"I'm busy. Give me half an hour."

He grabbed my elbow.

"I beg you to predispose yourself. Immediately."

"I don't understand. Predispose myself to what?"

"To giving me a few minutes. It's important to me."

"It's important to you," I repeated, continuing to make my way towards the stairs. "If it's important only to you, then to me, it's not that important."

He kept a hold on me as if tethered, planting his feet strangely: one with its toes out, the other with its toes in.

"Important to you too," he said. "You'll be happy. You'll get everything you want."

We were already halfway up the stairs.

"And what exactly are we going to talk about?" I asked.

"About the suitcase."

"So you're ready to answer my questions?"

"Let's stop walking and talk," he asked. "My legs work bad."

Ah, he's getting worked up, I thought. That's good—I like that.

"In half an hour," I said. "And let go of me, please. You're in my way."

"Yes," he said. "In your way. I want to be in your way. My conversation is urgent."

"How urgent could it be?" I objected. "There's no need to hurry. Half an hour. Or let's say an hour."

"No, no, immediately please. Everything depends on it. And it will be quick. Me to you, you to me. That's that."

We were already in the second floor hallway. I began to feel bad for him.

"Well, all right," I said. "Let's go to my room. Only it has to be quick."

"Yes, yes, of course, quick."

I led him to my room, sat down on the edge of the table and said,

"Tell me."

But he didn't start immediately. At first he looked around, hoping no doubt that the suitcase was lying somewhere within sight.

"The suitcase is not here," I said. "Now hurry up."

"Then I will sit down," he said, and sat in my chair. "I very much need this suitcase. What do you want for it?"

"I don't want anything for it. Prove that you have a right to it, and it's yours."

Luarvik L. Luarvik shook his head and said,

"No. I am not going to prove it. The briefcase is not mine. At first I didn't understand. But I thought a lot, and now I understand. Olaf stole the suitcase. I was ordered to find Olaf and tell him, 'Return what you took, Commandant two twenty-four.' I don't know what this means. I don't know what he took. And you keep saying 'suitcase'. This fools me. It is not a suitcase. It is a casing. Inside is a device. Before, I didn't know this. When I saw Olaf, I figured it out. Now I know: Olaf was not killed. Olaf died. From the device. The device is very dangerous. Its threat is to everyone. Everyone will become like Olaf, or perhaps an explosion will happen. Then it will be even worse. Do you understand why we need it quickly? Olaf was a fool, he died. We are smart, we won't die. Give me the suitcase quickly."

He babbled along in his flat tone, looking at me out of his right eye and then left eye in turn, tugging relentlessly at his empty sleeve. His face remained motionless, except that from time to time his thin eyebrows rose or fell. I watched him, thinking that his manners and grammar were the same as they had been before, but that his vocabulary had increased significantly. Luarvik had gotten better at speaking.

"Who are you anyway?" I asked.

"I'm an emigrant, a foreign specialist. Exile. Political refugee."

Yes, Luarvik had gotten better at talking. But who could have expected all this?

"An emigrant from where?"

"No need for such questions. I can't tell. I promised. It is not an enemy to your country."

"But you already told me that you're a Swede."

"A Swede? I never said that. I'm an emigrant, a political exile."

"Excuse me," I said. "An hour ago you told me you were a Swede. That you were a Swede for the most part. And now you deny it?"

"I don't know . . . I don't remember . . ." he muttered. "I don't feel good. I'm afraid. I must have the suitcase soon."

The more he urged me on, the less inclined I was to hurry. It was all clear to me: he was lying, and lying very badly.

"Where do you live?" I asked.

"I can't say."

"How did you get here?"

"Car."

"What model of car?"

"Model? . . . Black, large."

"You don't know the model of your own car?"

"I don't know, it's not mine."

"But you're a mechanic," I said gleefully. "How the hell can you be a mechanic—not to mention a driver—without knowing anything about cars?"

"Give me the suitcase, otherwise it will be bad."

"And what are you going to do with this suitcase?"

"Take it quickly away."

"To where? You know that an avalanche has blocked the road."

"It doesn't matter. I'll take it away. I will try to discharge it. If I can't I'll run away. Leave it there."

"Excellent," I said, springing up from the table. "Let's go."

"What?"

"In my car. I have a good car, a Moskvitch. We'll take the suitcase. We'll take it away, have a look at it."

He didn't move.

"It's no need for you. It's very dangerous."

"That's okay. I'll risk it . . . Ready?"

He sat without moving a muscle or saying a thing.

"Well, don't just sit there," I said. "If it's dangerous then we need to hurry."

"This won't do," he said finally. "Let's try another. If you won't give me the suitcase, then maybe you'll sell it. Ah?"

"What do you mean?" I asked, sitting down again at the table.

"I give you money, a lot of money. You give me the suitcase. No one will know, everyone is satisfied. You found a suitcase, I bought it. That's all."

"And how much will you give me?" I asked.

"A lot. As much as you want. Here."

He reached inside his jacket and pulled out a plump packet of bills. I had seen such a packet of notes only once in real life: at the state bank, where I had been working on a forgery case.

"How much is that?" I asked.

"Not enough? There's more."

He reached into his side pocket and pulled out another packet just like the other one and tossed it on the table in front of me.

"How much money is this?" I asked.

"What does it matter?" he asked, surprised. "It's all yours."

"It matters a lot. Do you know how much money this is?"

He kept quiet, his eyes focusing, then drifting apart.

"No. You don't. And where did you get it?"

"It's mine."

"Give it a rest, Luarvik. Who gave it to you? You came here with your pockets empty. It must have been Moses: no one else has that kind of money. Am I right?"

"You don't want the money?"

"Look here," I said. "I am going to confiscate this money, and then I'm going to charge you with attempting to bribe a government official. This is going to be a very bad thing for you, Luarvik . . . The only thing left for you to do is tell me the truth. Who are you?"

"You are taking the money?" Luarvik asked.

"I'm confiscating it."

"Confiscating . . . Excellent," he said. "Now where is the suitcase?"

"You don't understand what 'confiscating' means?" I asked. "Ask Moses . . . Come on, who are you?"

Without saying a word, he stood up and headed for the door. I grabbed the money and went after him. We walked through the hallway and then down the staircase.

"It's no use not giving me the suitcase," Luarvik said. "It won't be good for you."

"Don't threaten me," I reminded him.

"You will cause great misfortune."

"Stop lying," I said. "If you don't want to tell the truth that's your business. But you're already in it up to your ears, Luarvik, and now you've dragged the Moseses in with you. There's no easy way out anymore. The police will be here any minute, and when they are, you'll have no choice except to tell the truth . . . Stop! Not that way. Come with me."

I took him by the empty sleeve and led him to the owner's office. Then I called the owner and in his presence counted the money and wrote out a statement. The owner counted the money too—it was more than eighty thousand: what I would make over eight years of impeccable service—and signed the report.

All this time Luarvik stood off to one side, shifting awkwardly from foot to foot. He looked like a man who wanted to get out of there as soon as possible.

"Sign it," I said, handing him a pen.

He took the pen, looked at it intently and then laid it carefully on the table.

"No," he said. "I am leaving."

"As you wish," I said. "That won't change your situation."

He turned around immediately and left, banging his shoulder against the doorframe. The owner and I looked at one another.

"Why did he try to bribe you?" the owner asked. "What did he want?"

"The suitcase," I said.

"What suitcase?"

"Olaf's suitcase, the one that you have in your safe . . ." I took the key out and opened the safe. "This one."

"That's worth eighty thousand?" the owner asked with respect.

"Probably it's worth much more. This is turning out to be some murky business, Alek." I put the money in the safe, locked the heavy door again, and put the report in my pocket.

"Who is this Luarvik?" the owner asked thoughtfully. "Where did he get that kind of money?"

"Luarvik didn't have a penny when he came here. Moses must have given it to him. No one else could have."

The manager raised his fat finger, intending to say something, but then changed his mind. Instead, he rubbed his chubby chin, barked "Kaisa" vigorously and then walked out. I was left sitting in the office. I proceeded to think things over. I went carefully back over the smallest, most insignificant-seeming events which I had witnessed at the inn. I realized soon that I could remember a lot of them.

I remembered that at our first meeting Simone had been wearing a grey suit, and that at last night's party he'd been wearing a burgundy one, and that his cufflinks had featured yellow stones. I remembered that when Brun begged a cigarette off her uncle, he always pulled them from behind his right ear. I remembered that Kaisa had a small black birthmark on her right nostril; that when Du Barnstoker wielded his fork he raised his pinky finger elegantly; that the key to my room looked like the key to Olaf's room; and many other useless details like this. I excavated two whole gems from this dung heap. First, I remembered how, on the evening of the day before yesterday a snow-covered Olaf had stood in the middle of the hall with his black suitcase and looked around, as if expecting a more heartfelt welcome, and how he looked past me towards the curtained-off entrance to the Moseses' part of the inn, and how it had seemed to me that the curtain had been swaying—from a draft, I had assumed. Second, I remembered that while I'd been standing in line for the shower, I had seen Olaf and Moses descending the staircase hand in hand . . .

All this made me think that Olaf, Moses, and now Luarvik really did make up a single party—a party that did not want to let it be known that it was a single party. And if I remembered that I had discovered Moses in the memorial room next to my room five minutes before I found the note referring to the gangster and maniac on the ruined desk in my own room; and if I remembered that Moses's gold watch had been planted (clearly planted, and then removed again) in Hinkus's trunk . . . and if I remembered that Mrs. Moses was the one person, excepting maybe Kaisa, not in the dining room at the moment when Hinkus was overpowered and stuffed under the table . . . if I remembered all that, then the picture grew more curious.

Hinkus's statement that one of his trunks had been craftily turned into a piece of false baggage fit this picture well, as did the fact that Mrs. Moses had been the only person who had seen Hinkus's double personally. For it was impossible to say that Brun had seen Hinkus's double: the only thing she'd seen was his coat. She didn't know who'd been wearing that coat.

Of course, the picture still had quite a few blank and completely unclear spots. But at least the balance of power was

now clear: Hinkus on one side, and the Moseses, Olaf and Luarvik on the other. At the same time, judging by the complete
ridiculousness of Luarvik's actions and the openness with
which Moses had given him money, the situation did appear
to be approaching some sort of crisis . . . And then it entered
my head that maybe I'd locked Hinkus up in vain. In the coming confrontation it wouldn't be a bad idea to have an ally,
even one as questionable and obviously crooked as Hinkus.

So that's what I'll do, I thought. I'll sic the gangster and
maniac on them. After all, Moses probably thinks Hinkus is
still lying under the table. Let's see what he does when Hinkus
suddenly appears at the table for breakfast. As for who jumped
Hinkus and how they tied him up, not to mention who killed
Olaf, I decided not to think about those things for now. I
crumpled up my notes, put them in the ashtray and set them
on fire.

"Breakfast, everyone," Kaisa squeaked somewhere above
me. "Breakfast."

14.

Hinkus was already awake. He was standing in the middle of the room with his suspenders dangling, wiping his face with a large towel.

"Good morning," I said. "How do you feel?"

He glanced at me warily; his face was a little swollen, but for the most part he looked pretty good. All traces of the mad hunted ferret that I'd seen only a few hours ago had disappeared.

"Fine, more or less," he muttered. "Why am I locked in here?"

"You had a nervous breakdown," I explained. His face twitched slightly. "Nothing awful. The manager gave you an injection and locked you in so that no one would bother you. Want to go to breakfast?"

"I'm coming," he said. "I'll have my breakfast and get the hell out of here. And I'm taking my deposit back. A vacation in the mountains . . ." He balled the towel up and threw it aside. "Another vacation like this and I'd go nuts. Tuberculosis or no tuberculosis . . . Where's my coat, anyway? And my hat . . ."

"On the roof, probably," I said.

"On the roof . . ." he muttered, hoisting his suspenders. "On the roof . . ."

"Yes," I said. "I'm sorry, that's some bad luck . . . But we'll talk about it later."

I turned and walked towards the door.

"There's nothing to talk about!" he shouted angrily at my back.

No one was in the dining room yet. Kaisa was arranging the sandwich plates. I greeted her and chose a new seat for myself: back to the sideboard, face to the door, directly beside Du Barnstoker's seat. I had barely sat down when Simone came in wearing a thick, colorful sweater. He was freshly shaven, with puffy red eyes.

"What a night, Inspector," he said. "I didn't get even five hours' sleep. My nerves were a wreck. I can't get rid of this smell of dead flesh—that pharmaceutical stench, you know what I mean? Like formaldehyde . . ." He sat down, picked out a sandwich, and then looked at me. "Did you find anything?" he asked.

"That depends on what you mean," I said.

"Aha," he said, and laughed uncertainly. "You don't look well."

"Every man wears the face he deserves," I said, at the exact second that the Barnstokers came in. They looked fresh as daisies. The uncle sported an aster in his buttonhole; the dome of his bald head shone in the midst of silver-gray curls; Brun was wearing glasses, as before, and her nose was still brazenly raised. Uncle rubbed his hands together as he approached his seat, looking searchingly at me.

"Good morning, Inspector," he sang gently. "What an awful night! Good morning, Mr. Simone. Don't you agree?"

"Hi," muttered the kid.

"What I wouldn't give for some cognac," Simone said with a sort of wistfulness. "But that wouldn't be right, would it? Or would it?"

"I don't know, to be honest," said Du Barnstoker. "I wouldn't risk it."

"How about you, Inspector?" Simone said.

I shook my head and sipped the coffee that Kaisa had set in front of me.

"Too bad," said Simone. "Then I would have had a drink."

"And how are we doing this morning, my dear inspector?" Du Barnstoker asked.

"The investigation is on track," I said. "The police have the key in hand. Many keys. The entire ring, in fact."

Simone started cackling as usual, but then immediately made a serious face.

"No doubt we'll have to spend all day indoors," said Du Barnstoker. "No leaving, I assume."

"Why not?" I replied. "Do whatever you want. The more so, the better."

"Escape is futile, anyway," said Simone. "There's the avalanche. We're locked in here—for a while, too. It's an ideal situation for the police. I, of course, could escape via the cliffs . . ."

"Then why don't you?" I asked.

"In the first place, because I can't get to the cliffs through the snow. In the second, because what would I do once I'd gotten there? . . . Listen, gentlemen," he said. "Why don't we take a walk down the road—let's see for ourselves what Bottleneck looks like . . ."

"You have no objection, Inspector?" Du Barnstoker asked.

"No," I said, as the Moseses came in. They looked fresh as daisies too. That is to say, Madame Moses looked like a daisy, like a peach, like the sun itself. As for Moses, he was the same withered old rutabaga as before. He made his way past us without saying hello to anyone, gulping from his mug, and then slumped into his chair to stare dismally at the sandwiches in front of him.

The crystalline voice of Mrs. Moses rang out. "Good morning, gentlemen!"

I glanced at Simone, who was glancing at Mrs. Moses, somewhat suspiciously, it seemed. Then he shrugged spasmodically and grabbed his coffee.

"What a charming morning," Mrs. Moses continued. "Look how sunny it is! Pity poor Olaf that he isn't alive to see it!"

"We'll all be there someday," Moses barked suddenly.

"Amen," concluded Du Barnstoker politely.

I looked at Brun. The girl was hunched over with her nose buried in her mug. The door opened again and Luarvik L. Luarvik appeared, accompanied by the owner. The owner smiled gloomily.

"Good morning, ladies and gentlemen," he said. "Please allow me to introduce Mr. Luarvik Luarvik, who joined us last night. He suffered an accident on the road, and naturally we would not refuse him our hospitality."

Mr. Luarvik Luarvik indeed looked like a man who had suffered a terrible accident and was very much in need of hospitality. The owner had to take him by the elbow and literally push him into my old seat next to Simone.

"Very nice to meet you, Luarvik," Moses croaked. "There are no strangers here, Luarvik—make yourself at home."

"Yes," said Luarvik, looking with one eye at me, and with the other at Simone. "Wonderful weather we're having. A real winter . . ."

"Nonsense, Luarvik," Moses said. "Less talk, more eating. You look exhausted . . . Simone, would you mind telling the one about the maître d' again? He ate someone's filet, if I remember right . . ."

At that moment, Hinkus finally appeared. He walked in and immediately stopped. Simone started telling the story about the maître d' again, and while he was explaining that said person had not eaten any filet, that in fact quite the opposite had happened, Hinkus stood in the doorway, and I watched him, trying at the same time to keep an eye on the Moseses. I did, but that didn't get me anywhere. Mrs. Moses ate her cookies and cream and listened admiringly to the troublemaking bore. Mr. Moses did turn one bloodshot eye in Hinkus's direction—but he did so with complete indifference, and then returned to his mug. Hinkus, on the other hand, was having a hard time controlling his expression.

At first he looked completely dazed, as if someone had hit him over the head with an oar. Then his face became clearly overcome with joy, a sort of excitement—he even smiled suddenly, just like a child. Then his smile turned into an evil grin and he stepped forward, clenching his fists. But to my great surprise, he wasn't looking at the Moseses. He was looking at the Barnstokers: first in confusion, then with relief and excitement, and finally with spite and a sort of gleeful malice. He caught me looking at him and relaxed slightly, lowering his gaze as he went over to his seat.

"How are you feeling, Mr. Hinkus?" Du Barnstoker asked, bending forward considerately. "The air here . . ."

Hinkus glared at him with insane yellow eyes.

"I'm all right," he answered, sitting down. "But then how about you—how are you feeling?"

Du Barnstoker leaned back in his chair in surprise.

"Me? Thank you . . ." He looked first at me, then at Brun. "Perhaps I have said something wrong . . . touched on . . . In that case, I beg . . ."

"Didn't work out, did it?" Hinkus continued, furiously stuffing a napkin into his collar. "Fell through, didn't it, old man?"

Du Barnstoker was in a state of complete confusion. All

talk at the table had stopped, everyone was looking at him and Hinkus.

"Really, I'm afraid . . ." The old magician clearly had no idea what to do. "I was only inquiring after your health, nothing more . . ."

"Of course, of course, we'll drop it," Hinkus responded.

He took a big sandwich in both hands, maneuvered a corner into his mouth and proceeded to chew on it without looking at anyone else.

"There's no need to be rude!" Brun said suddenly.

Hinkus glanced briefly at her and then immediately looked away.

"Brun, my child," said Du Barnstoker.

"B-blowhard!" Brun said, striking her knife against her plate. "Maybe if you drank less . . ."

"Gentlemen, gentlemen!" the owner said. "All this is foolishness!"

"Don't worry, Snevar," Du Barnstoker said quickly. "This is nothing more than a little misunderstanding . . . Nerves are strained . . . The events of the night . . ."

"Didn't you hear me?" Brun asked menacingly, pointing her black lenses at Hinkus.

"Ladies and gentlemen!" the owner interjected authoritatively. "Ladies and gentlemen, if I could have your attention. I am not going to talk about the tragic events of last night. I understand: yes, nerves are strained. But let us remember, first of all, that the investigation into the unfortunate fate of Olaf Andvarafors is safely in the hands of Inspector Glebsky, who, by a happy coincidence, happened to be in our midst. Secondly, we must not be enervated by the fact that we find ourselves cut off from the outside world . . ."

Hinkus stopped chewing and raised his head.

"Our cellars are full, gentlemen!" the owner continued

vehemently. "Every imaginable provision, and even a few unimaginable ones, are at your disposal. And I am sure that
when a rescue party breaks through the blockage and reaches
us in a few days, it will find us . . ."

"What blockage?" Hinkus asked loudly, looking around
wide-eyed. "What the hell is this?"

"Yes, please excuse me," the owner said, bringing a hand
to his forehead. "I completely forgot that a few of our guests
might not know about this event. To be brief: at ten o'clock
last night, an avalanche blocked the Bottleneck and cut off
telephone service."

Silence descended over the table. Everyone was chewing
and staring at their plates. Hinkus sat with his mouth open—
once again, he appeared completely dumbfounded. A melancholy Luarvik L. Luarvik chewed on a lemon, biting into it
skin and all. Yellow juice ran down his narrow chin and onto
his jacket. My jaw was cramping, I took a sip of coffee and
announced:

"If I might add the following: two small gangs of lowlifes
have, for some reason, chosen this hotel as the place to settle
their accounts with one another. In my current informal ca-
pacity, I can take only limited steps. For example, I can gather
evidence for when the official police from Mur get here. This
evidence has, for the most part, been gathered already, although I would be very grateful to any citizen who gives the
investigation any new information. Furthermore I want to
make it known to all good citizens that they are out of danger
and free to conduct themselves in whatever way they please.
As for those persons who make up the abovementioned gangs,
I advise them to cease their activities, so as not to worsen their
already hopeless situation. I would like to remind you that
our isolation from the outside world is relative. Some of you
here already know that two hours ago I availed myself of an

offer of Mr. Snevar's and sent a message via carrier pigeon to
Mur. Now I expect the arrival of a police plane at any hour,
and for that reason remind those persons who are involved
in criminal activities that timely confession and repentance
would significantly improve their lots. Thank you for your attention, everyone."

"How interesting!" Mrs. Moses exclaimed delightedly.
"That means that there are bandits in our midst? Oh, Inspector, please give us a hint! We'll guess it!"

I glanced over at the owner. Alek Snevar had turned his
expansive back on his guests in order to carefully wipe the
shot glasses on the sideboard.

Conversation did not resume. Spoons clinked quietly in
their cups, Mr. Moses breathed noisily over his mug, drill-
ing his eyes into everyone in turn. No one was giving themselves away, though anyone who had reason to think about
their fate was thinking about it. I had let a healthy ferret into
this chicken coop, and now just had to wait for something to
happen.

Du Barnstoker was the first to stand up.

"Ladies and gentlemen!" he said. "I call upon all good citizens to put their skis on and go on a little excursion. The sun,
the fresh air, the snow and a clear conscience will surely help
fortify and calm us. Brun, my child, come along."

One after another the guests pushed their chairs back and
got up from the table to leave the room. Simone offered his
arm to Mrs. Moses—apparently, his memories of the previous
night had vanished utterly under the influence of the sunny
morning and a thirst for sensual pleasure. Mr. Moses pulled
Luarvik L. Luarvik up from the table and stood him up; Luarvik followed behind him, shuffling his feet as he chewed
mechanically on his lemon.

Only Hinkus was left at the table. He was eating intently,

as if he intended to fill himself with enough fuel to last a long time. The owner helped Kaisa gather up the dishes.

"Well, Hinkus?" I said. "Shall we talk?"

"About what?" he said gloomily as he ate an egg with pepper.

"About everything," I said. "As you can see, you won't be going anywhere anytime soon. And there's no need to hang around on the roof anymore, right?"

"We've got nothing to talk about," Hinkus said grimly. "I don't know anything about your case."

"About what case?" I asked.

"About the murder! What else . . ."

"But there's still the Hinkus case," I said. "Are you done? If so, let's go. We'll go to the pool room: it's sunny in there, and no one will disturb us."

He didn't say anything. He chewed his egg, swallowed, wiped his mouth with his napkin and stood up.

"Alek," I said to the manager. "Do me a favor, come down and sit in the lobby where you were yesterday—understand?"

"Understood," said the manager. "You got it."

He quickly wiped his hands off on the towel, and went out. I opened the door to the billiard room and let Hinkus go in first. He entered and stopped, standing with his hands in his pockets, chewing a match. I took one of the chairs lining the wall, stood it in the middle of the sunlight and said, "Sit." Hinkus hesitated a second, then sat and immediately squinted. The sunlight was in his face.

"An old police trick," he mumbled bitterly.

"That's the nature of the job," I said, and sat in front of him on the edge of the billiard table, which was out of the sun. "So, Hinkus, what happened in there between you and Barnstoker?"

"What about Barnstoker? What could have happened

between us? Nothing happened. I don't know anything about him."

"You wrote the note threatening him?"

"I didn't write any note. But I will write a complaint. For torturing a sick man . . ."

"Listen, Hinkus. In an hour or two the police will fly in. The experts are coming. I have your note in my pocket. It won't be too hard for them to determine that you wrote it. Why aren't you talking?"

With a quick movement he shifted the match he was chewing on from one corner of his mouth to the other. Kaisa was clattering dishes in the dining room, singing something out of tune in her thin voice.

"I don't know anything about a note," Hinkus said finally.

"Stop lying, Finch!" I shouted. "I know all about you! You're in trouble, Finch. And if you're looking to get off under section 72, you'd better get in line with paragraph D! Make a frank confession before the official investigation begins . . . well? How about it?"

He spat out the match, rummaged around in his pockets and pulled out a crumpled pack of cigarettes. Then he brought the pack up to his mouth, pulled a cigarette out of it with his lips, and thought.

"Well?" I said.

"You're confusing me with someone else," Hinkus answered. "Someone named Finch. I'm not Finch. I'm Hinkus."

I leaped off the pool table and held the gun under his nose.

"What about that? Do you recognize that? Is it yours? Speak up!"

"I don't know anything about it," he said grimly. "Why are you harassing me?"

I sat back down on the table, lay the gun next to me on the felt and lit a cigarette.